"Emma Diamond and her . . . friends Sophie and Mary-lou may not be experts at the table, but they're determined to trump someone's ace in this quiet Houston suburb. A charming and clever debut by Honor Hartman."

—*Joan Hess, author of the Claire Malloy
and Maggody series

"Hartman plays this hand . . . with aplomb, and bridge players and mystery fans alike will want to see what she deals out next." —*Richmond-Times Dispatch*

"A terrific amateur sleuth series. The story line is well plotted and contains quite a few twists and tricks as Emma bids on who killed the despot."

—*Midwest Book Review*

"Understanding the actual game play is not necessary to enjoy the mystery. If you're interested in learning the game, the author includes some good resources and tips at the end of the book to get you started. The mystery is quite interesting, and the author manages to throw in a few good twists toward the end. *On the Slam* is a good start to what promises to be an entertaining series." —*CA Reviews*

"A good yarn . . . I look forward to seeing where Ms. Hartman takes the series." —*Gumshoe*

"Readers who are not bridge players needn't shy away from this cozy, which is populated with likable characters. [*On the Slam*] will provide an afternoon of fun."

—*Romantic Times*

THE UNKINDEST CUT

♠ ♥ ♦ ♣

A BRIDGE CLUB MYSTERY

Honor Hartman

AN OBSIDIAN MYSTERY

OBSIDIAN
Published by New American Library, a division of
Penguin Group (USA) Inc., 375 Hudson Street,
New York, New York 10014, USA
Penguin Group (Canada), 90 Eglinton Avenue East, Suite 700, Toronto,
Ontario M4P 2Y3, Canada (a division of Pearson Penguin Canada Inc.)
Penguin Books Ltd., 80 Strand, London WC2R 0RL, England
Penguin Ireland, 25 St. Stephen's Green, Dublin 2,
Ireland (a division of Penguin Books Ltd.)
Penguin Group (Australia), 250 Camberwell Road, Camberwell, Victoria 3124,
Australia (a division of Pearson Australia Group Pty. Ltd.)
Penguin Books India Pvt. Ltd., 11 Community Centre, Panchsheel Park,
New Delhi - 110 017, India
Penguin Group (NZ), 67 Apollo Drive, Rosedale, North Shore 0632,
New Zealand (a division of Pearson New Zealand Ltd.)
Penguin Books (South Africa) (Pty.) Ltd., 24 Sturdee Avenue,
Rosebank, Johannesburg 2196, South Africa

Penguin Books Ltd., Registered Offices:
80 Strand, London WC2R 0RL, England

First published by Obsidian, an imprint of New American Library,
a division of Penguin Group (USA) Inc.

First Printing, June 2008
10 9 8 7 6 5 4 3 2 1

PUBLISHER'S NOTE
This is a work of fiction. Names, characters, places, and incidents either are
the product of the author's imagination or are used fictitiously, and any resemblance to actual persons, living or dead, business establishments, events, or
locales is entirely coincidental.

The publisher does not have any control over and does not assume any
responsibility for author or third-party Web sites or their content.

Acknowledgments

Thanks are due, as always, to several people who contribute in important ways to the process. Kerry Donovan, my editor, has been supportive and encouraging; Nancy Yost, my agent, takes care of the business end capably and cheerfully; and my never-failing support team, Tejas Englesmith, Julie Wray Herman, and Patricia Orr, continue to be there whenever I need them. Finally, a word to my friends at Murder by the Book in Houston: thank you for your unfailing efforts to get the word out about my books. Your enthusiasm and effort are much appreciated.

Author's Note

The bridge retreat depicted in the pages of this novel is entirely a product of the author's imagination. Any resemblance to persons, places, or events is entirely coincidental. The characters and events were designed to suit the demands of the plot and nothing more.

Chapter 1

I stared at my hand. Was it strong enough for the course of action I was attempting?

There was only one way to find out. I hesitated a moment longer, then clicked on the button to bid six hearts.

I half expected my computer opponent to double, and when that didn't happen, I grinned. I had been playing this computer bridge game for a little over six months now, and I had yet to understand all its vagaries of bidding.

Olaf stretched and yawned in my lap, his claws kneading the side of my thigh. Thank goodness I had clipped his nails yesterday, or I would have had little spots of blood all over my sweatpants by the time he was through. I rubbed his head, and his purring hit overdrive.

Hilda, my other cat, contemplated me sleepily from her napping spot on the desk by my computer. I had long ago given up trying to dissuade the two cats from climbing all over me and my computer when I was trying to work—or play bridge, which I had to admit happened a lot more frequently than work these days. We had settled on a compromise—Olaf in my lap,

Hilda on a comfy pad on the desk where she could keep an eye on Olaf and me.

I focused my attention on the computer. It had made the opening lead, and now my dummy partner's hand was revealed. I quickly counted the points in it, and I grinned again. With my eighteen high card points and dummy's thirteen, we had enough for slam.

Before playing out of dummy's hand to continue the first round, I made some quick calculations. I could easily make six hearts, but only if the king of spades was held by my left-hand opponent. The finesse had to work.

I began to play the game, clicking away with my right hand while my left continued rubbing Olaf's head. The spade king fell as I hoped, assuring me of victory. I was about to click on the next card when a voice called from downstairs.

"Emma! Where are you?"

"In my office," I yelled back. "Come on up." I grimaced when Olaf dug his claws into my leg as he prepared to jump to the floor. Even clipped, those claws were sharp enough to penetrate the skin when twelve pounds of cat decided to use my leg as a launching pad.

I finished the game and shut down the computer just as my next-door neighbor and best friend, Sophie Parker, appeared in the doorway. "Morning, Emma," she said. "Did you win?" She tilted her head toward the computer.

"Morning, and yes, I did," I said, examining her from head to toe. I marveled as always at the fact that she almost never appeared anything other than immaculately turned out. Ruefully, I glanced down at my ratty old sweatpants and faded Rice T-shirt. My hair was probably sticking up in spikes, not to mention the hated cowlick I had never been able to conquer.

Sophie's blond head shone, her hair neatly pulled back into a sleek ponytail. Her sweats, made of iridescent, multicolored silk material, probably cost more than the most expensive dress in my closet. Then there were the running shoes—shoes that were never used for running, of course. Sophie was elegantly thin, and though she reputedly spent time on a treadmill every day, I had yet to see this fabled machine.

"What is it, Emma?" Sophie asked, smiling.

I shook my head. "Nothing. I'm wondering, yet again, how you always look like you just stepped out of the Neiman Marcus catalog."

She giggled at that comment. "You do say the sweetest things. But I guess that's what best friends are for."

I couldn't help smiling back at her. We had been best friends for a long time, ever since she was four and I was twelve. We had grown up next door to each other in another part of Houston, and both of us had parents who were flaky in vastly different ways. Sophie and I, and my younger brother, Jake, had looked out for one another, especially since the so-called adults in our lives were too busy with other things to pay much attention to their children.

"Don't you get tired of sitting at that computer?" Sophie asked. "I swear, you're playing bridge on it every time I come over lately."

"It passes the time," I said, "and it does help me with my bridge game."

"You are playing very well these days," Sophie said, "so I suppose the computer does help." Olaf twined himself around her legs, and she reached down and

scratched his head. Sophie had two dogs, Boston terri-
ers, and Olaf loved rubbing himself on her legs. No
doubt it drove Mavis and Martha crazy when their
mommy came home smelling of cat, and that's exactly
what Olaf intended, I was sure. On the few occasions
when my cats and Sophie's dogs had shared the same
space, they had not been happy about it.

"Thank you." Sophie played very well, too, though
I didn't think she worked at it the way I did. Some
people are naturally good at many things without a
lot of effort, and Sophie was one of those people. If
I didn't love her so much, I could have cheerfully
killed her on many occasions.

I glanced at my watch. It was a few minutes past
eight thirty. "How about some coffee?" I asked as I
led the way downstairs.

"Sounds good," Sophie replied. "And do you have
any of that yummy coffee cake left?" Then she sighed.
"I really shouldn't have any, but it's so wonderful I
simply can't resist."

I laughed as she followed me into the kitchen. "Yes,
I do have some left. I keep telling Marylou she doesn't
have to bring coffee cake all the time, but she never
listens to me."

"Thank goodness she doesn't," Sophie said as she
helped herself to coffee from the pot on the counter.
"I like being spoiled."

I retrieved some dessert plates from the cabinet, cut
generous slices of coffee cake for each of us, and set
them on the table. I poured myself some coffee and
sat down across from Sophie.

"Have you talked to Marylou this morning?" Sophie asked as she pinched a piece of coffee cake and
popped it into her mouth.

"No," I said, "but now that her friend is visiting, I'm sure she's busy with her."

Marylou Lockridge, a widow in her mid-sixties, was my neighbor on the other side. In the past few months, since I had moved into this house, Sophie and I had grown very close to Marylou. We shared coffee every morning, usually in my kitchen, since my house was between theirs, and this morning it felt distinctly odd not to have Marylou's motherly presence at the table with us.

"At least we'll see her at lunch today," Sophie said. "I wonder what her friend is like."

Marylou had invited us both to lunch today at her house. She wanted us to meet her friend, about whom she had told us next to nothing.

"I'm curious, too," I admitted. "I wonder why Marylou hasn't said much about her."

"Maybe she simply hasn't thought about it, not realizing that we're both dying of curiosity," Sophie said. She ate the last morsel of her coffee cake, even as she gazed longingly at the remaining piece on the counter.

"Go for it," I said, trying not to laugh. "With your metabolism, you'll burn it off very quickly."

"I suppose," Sophie said, her tone indicating that she actually doubted it. I just rolled my eyes. The girl had the metabolism of a hyperactive chipmunk, and she could eat anything and not gain more than an ounce or two. She got up from her chair and put the last piece of coffee cake on her plate.

I, on the other hand, had only to look at chocolate, and I immediately put on two pounds—despite the fact that I went for an extended walk along the nearby bayou at least five times a week. *Make that four,* I amended silently, remembering that I had decided to skip my walk this morning in favor of computer bridge.

Sophie broke the piece in two and put half of it on my plate. I sighed. At this rate I never would lose the ten pounds I really ought to shed. Marylou's coffee cake, like anything she baked, was heavenly and completely irresistible.

"Did Marylou tell you she had a surprise for us?"

I frowned at Sophie. "No, I don't remember her saying anything about a surprise. Did she tell you what it might be?"

Sophie shrugged. "I don't think she actually said 'surprise,' come to think of it." She thought for a moment before continuing. "I think maybe what she really said was she had something she wanted to ask us, and she sounded kind of excited."

"And that's all she said to you?"

"Yeah," Sophie replied. She finished her last bite of coffee cake.

"Then I guess we'll just have to wait until lunch to find out," I said. "She said twelve thirty, didn't she?"

Sophie nodded before sipping from her coffee.

"Then I have plenty of time to do some house-cleaning before I have to clean myself up," I said. "My hair is really beginning to get out of control. I should make an appointment to have it cut."

Sophie eyed me critically. "Yes, Emma, you could use a good cut. I wish you'd let me make an appointment for you with my hairdresser."

Considering that Sophie usually spent about 150 dollars when she had her hair done, I wasn't certain I really wanted an introduction to her stylist. It wasn't the amount, because I could have afforded it. My late husband, Baxter Diamond, had left me handsomely provided for, but something in me rebelled at spending that much money on my hair. Sophie had told me more than once that this was a distinctly unfeminine attitude.

Easily interpreting my lack of response to her offer, Sophie laughed. "I guess I should know better by now. But one of these days I'm going to kidnap you and take you myself. You ought to let yourself be pampered sometimes, Emma."

"If I want pampering," I said, "I can think of many ways to pamper myself other than by spending that much money on my head."

"Like your expensive wardrobe?" Sophie arched an eyebrow.

"Ha-ha," I made a face at her. "You might like to wear the gross national product of Uruguay on your back, but I prefer to pamper myself in other ways. Mostly books."

Sophie shook her head. "You and your first editions."

And Baxter's, I added silently. I kept adding to the collection of first-edition mysteries that had been Baxter's pride and joy. For a moment the tears threatened to come, and I turned my head slightly away from Sophie to get myself under control.

"Honey, I'm sorry," Sophie said. "I really am a cat sometimes, and you know I didn't mean anything by what I said."

"I know," I said, reaching across the table to accept the hand she proffered. I returned her quick squeeze of affection, then withdrew my hand and sat back in my chair. "It just hits me sometimes."

"It hasn't even been a year yet," Sophie said, her voice soft. "It takes time."

I nodded. Time—day after day, night after night, without my beloved husband. Most of the time I did okay, but every once in a while, the pain hit me so hard I couldn't do anything except curl up in a tight little ball on the bed and cry myself to exhaustion.

Olaf would scrunch up beside me, watching me anxiously, occasionally licking my hand, while Hilda would rub her head against mine. Without them, and without Sophie and my brother and his partner, I think I would have gone completely mad. Marylou was another source of great comfort.

"How do you think we should dress for lunch next door?" I said.

Sophie shrugged. "I don't think we need to be too formal. I mean, good gracious, it's just lunch at Marylou's."

"Yes," I said, "but she's inviting us to meet her friend, so I think we should make an effort for her sake."

Sophie leveled one of her looks at me, and I almost turned red. It wasn't Sophie that Marylou had to worry about. I held up a hand. "Okay, message received. I know you'll be dressed appropriately. But what should I wear? I'm sure you have a suggestion or two."

Sophie smiled. "One of these days I'm going to take you shopping, honey, and we're going to update that wardrobe of yours. But for today, I think you should wear that lilac sheath with your pearls. It's understated, not too dressy, and it's a lovely color on you."

"Thank you," I said. Most of the time I preferred to run around in casual clothes, but I did like to look nice when the occasion demanded. I had simply never spent as much time on my appearance as Sophie did. But then I wasn't beautiful like she was. People often mistook her for a model.

"I suppose I should go home and let you get busy with your cleaning," Sophie said. She rose from her chair. "I'll see you at Marylou's." She waved a hand at me as she exited through the back door.

I spent the next two hours cleaning. First I tackled the bathrooms; next I vacuumed my bedroom and most of the upstairs, and I ended with some dusting. By the time I finished, I was hot, bedraggled, and dusty. A cool shower soon revived me, and I had enough time to dress and do my makeup so that I didn't have to rush.

At twenty-eight minutes past twelve I walked out my front door, taking care to lock it after reassuring myself that I had put my keys in my purse. Sophie answered the door for Marylou, informing me that our hostess was in the kitchen. "Her friend hasn't come down yet," Sophie said, shutting the door behind me.

I followed her into the living room, and Sophie put out a hand to restrain me when I would have continued toward the kitchen.

"What is it?" I said.

Sophie glanced in the direction of the kitchen, and when she answered me, she lowered her voice to little more than a whisper. "Marylou told me her friend can come across as a bit strange, but she wants us to know that she's really a nice person, once you get to know her."

Looking askance at Sophie, I was about to reply when someone spoke from behind us in loud, angry tones.

"I wish he was dead. He's making everything so difficult, just to spite me. I ought to kill him myself."

Chapter 2

Sophie and I stared at each other, her eyes widening in surprise along with mine. Slowly we turned to look at the woman who had uttered those unsettling words.

She wasn't paying attention to anyone around her. She was peering into the distance, and I wasn't certain she had actually seen us. As I stared at her, I thought at first she was talking to herself, because her hands were empty, her arms hanging loosely by her side.

Then she shifted her head slightly, and in her right ear I spotted one of those ear gadgets I had seen other people wear. They looked uncomfortable to me, and I couldn't imagine wanting to wear a phone in my ear for any length of time. I didn't like using my own regular cell phone to begin with, and I hardly ever turned it on. My late husband had insisted I have one in case of emergency, but luckily I hadn't had to use it for one so far.

Abruptly the woman focused on Sophie and me, and she stared hard at both of us. She told the person on the other end of the conversation that she had to go, and then she reached up and pulled the device from her ear.

Not smiling, she stepped forward and held out her

hand. "Paula Trowbridge. How do you do?" I supposed she was going to pretend that we hadn't heard her threatening remarks.

Sophie and I introduced ourselves, and I continued to examine Paula Trowbridge as discreetly as I could. She was around fifty, probably a couple of years on the other side of it. That made her a bit more than ten years older than I and twenty years older than Sophie. Her face had a hard set to it, and the severely bleached blond hair did nothing to soften her look. She was rail thin, bronzed from many hours in the sun, and a good two inches taller than my own five seven.

Marylou came into the living room before we had much chance to do more than introduce ourselves. "Good, you've met," she said with a beaming smile. "It's so nice to have you all together with me." She turned to Sophie and me. "I've known Paula for nearly thirty years, you know."

"Marylou's one of the few people who've stuck by me," Paula said, frowning. "People are always letting me down. I don't know what it is. I spend so much time trying to be a good friend, and then my so-called new best friend stops returning my calls."

"That's a shame," I said, trying to keep my tone neutral. Sophie stared at Paula, one eyebrow quirked upward in an expression I knew all too well. I could read Sophie's mind, and I hoped she would keep her mouth shut until we were alone.

"I'm such a giving person," Paula said, not acknowledging my response. Her expression turned tragically woebegone. "It's so hard sometimes."

"Yes, dear, I know," Marylou said in a tone full of sympathy. I detected signs of strain in her face, however. If Paula had been carrying on in this vein ever since she arrived yesterday, no wonder Marylou was feeling it. "But you're here with me now, and you've got two *new* friends. I know you'll enjoy getting to know Sophie and Emma. And like I told you, they're both excellent bridge players."

Paula didn't appear too thrilled over that last sentence. "God, I'm so sick of bridge sometimes, I could just scream." Eyes narrowed, she regarded Sophie and me. "My husband is Avery Trowbridge." She paused a moment. "Surely you've heard of him." I hadn't thought it possible for her facial expression to turn any more sour, but now it did.

I had no idea who the heck Avery Trowbridge was, but evidently Sophie recognized the name. "Of course," she said. "He's one of the more outstanding bridge teachers—and players—in the world. I've often wondered what it would be like to play with him."

Paula had relaxed slightly at Sophie's first sentence, but then she frowned. "He's a complete bastard to play with," she said. The bitterness in her voice made me uncomfortable. "He's incredible in bed, though." Here she paused to smile, but that faded as she continued. "At the bridge table, he's a complete and utter bastard. He doesn't care how he humiliates you. He won't play bridge with me anymore. Can you believe that?"

At this point I was ready to tell Marylou I had a splitting headache, because I didn't think I could take much more of Paula's negativity. She wore unhappiness like perfume, and I almost thought I smelled it emanating from her in waves.

"That's enough of that, dear," Marylou said, her tone just the tiniest bit sharp. "There's no point in upsetting yourself. You'll give yourself another migraine if you don't watch out." She patted Paula on the arm, and Paula actually had the grace to look abashed.

"Sorry," she muttered.

Sophie and I exchanged swift glances. I didn't think either one of us had any doubts as to why Paula never managed to keep her friends. I had to wonder how Marylou had stood her for thirty years if she had always been like this. Marylou was such a kind, motherly soul, though, she probably felt sorry for Paula.

"I thought we'd have lunch in the kitchen, if y'all don't mind," Marylou said. "It's just so much cozier, I think." She turned and led us out of the living room.

"Oh, yes," I said, trying to put as much enthusiasm in my voice as I could muster. "Your kitchen is always so inviting, Marylou. With the most heavenly smells."

"Marylou is a wonderful cook," Paula said. "I'm not very good at it, though. Every time I try anything more complicated than scrambled eggs or a hamburger, the results are disastrous. I just don't have the knack. I don't know how Marylou does it."

"Oh, lots of practice," Marylou said, keeping things light. "I do love it so." She laughed as she looked down at her body. "And I think it shows. I'm too fond of sampling my own efforts, I guess." She pointed us to our seats, and we sat down at the table. It was very prettily set with festive napkins in bright colors, and a lovely centerpiece of brightly hued flowers.

Marylou was very much on the plump side, but she was fairly active and not in great danger of becoming *too* plump.

"Your food is simply too hard to resist," Sophie said, leaning forward, her elbows on the table on either side of her plate. "I really have to fight with myself not to gobble up everything in sight when I'm at your house." She giggled. "Otherwise I'd have to live on my treadmill."

Paula sighed heavily. "I *do* have to live on mine," she said. "Because I have absolutely no willpower where food is concerned. I can look at a slice of cheesecake, and I feel like I've suddenly gained five pounds."

"I know how you feel," I said. I tried to give Paula a friendly smile. "I have the same problem. I love good food, and with Marylou living next door to me, there's always something wonderful to try. Marylou spoils us terribly."

"I wish someone would spoil me," Paula said. "Basil used to, but then I screwed that up royally." Her mouth twisted in a bitter grimace.

"Who's Basil?" Sophie asked.

"Basil Dumont," Paula said, and Sophie's eyes widened in surprise. "My first husband."

I tilted my head sideways a bit, watching Sophie. Seeing my gesture, she answered. "Basil Dumont is pretty well-known in bridge circles, but he's not really in Avery Trowbridge's league. Avery's kind of a bridge superstar."

"Oh, I see," I said. Paula evidently moved in an exalted social sphere, at least as far as the bridge world was concerned.

"If I had known then what I know now," Paula said with a heavy sigh, "I can tell you I sure wouldn't have left Basil for Avery. No matter how good Avery is in bed, it's just not worth it. Basil took care of me."

Maybe Paula had turned into this bitter, sad person after her second marriage, I thought, trying to be charitable. Otherwise, I was having a really hard time imagining either of her husbands wanting to stay married to her.

"Now, dear," Marylou said while carrying a tureen of soup to the table. She began ladling a fragrant tomato-basil concoction into our soup bowls. "It doesn't do much good to look backward. You've made your bed, so to speak, and you need to resign yourself to that."

"The soup smells wonderful," I said, and the words were hardly out of my mouth before Paula started speaking.

"But that's where you're wrong, Marylou," Paula said. "I *can* go back, and I *have* to. If I don't, I know I'll go right out of my mind."

I caught Sophie rolling her eyes, and I could hear the words as clearly as if she had spoken them aloud. *That train's already left the station, honey.*

I tried not to react and choke on the delicious soup I had just spooned into my mouth. Swallowing hastily, I reached for my napkin to wipe my lips.

Marylou came back to the table and sat down. Picking up her spoon, she regarded Paula. "Now, what on earth do you mean by that, Paula? How can you go back?"

Paula's self-satisfied smile lit up her face. "Because Basil wants me back, that's how. He still loves me—I know he does—and all I have to do is get Avery to agree to a divorce."

"Basil has actually told you this?" Marylou asked, while Sophie and I looked back and forth at her and Paula like spectators at Wimbledon.

Paula shrugged. "Well, not in so many words." The light in her face had dimmed for a moment, but now it came blazing back. "But I know him so well, you see, and I can tell what he's thinking, even if he won't say the words straight out. He wants me back. I know he does."

It seemed not to matter what anyone else thought. Paula had evidently convinced herself, and even Marylou's obvious skepticism didn't deflate her.

"My goodness," Marylou said as she jumped up from her chair. "I forgot the tea." From the nearby counter she retrieved a pitcher, the sides specked with moisture. She went around the table, filling our glasses.

I thought about trying to change the subject, but I figured it was probably a lost cause. From even the brief acquaintance I had with Paula, I decided that any conversation in which she took part would revolve mostly around her.

Marylou settled back into her place. "Now everything becomes clear." She fixed Paula with a basilisk stare. "Come clean, Paula. You want me along to help you with some harebrained scheme to win Basil back, right?"

Paula flushed. "I wish you wouldn't put it like that. You make me sound so self-centered, and you know I'm not really like that."

If she were waiting for Marylou to reassure her with a denial of those words, she was evidently going to wait a long time. Marylou just kept staring at her, and Paula began to wilt.

Taking pity on her, I decided to venture a question. "Along on what, Marylou? Are you going somewhere with Paula?"

"I was," Marylou said, "but now I'm not so sure."

"Please say you'll still come," Paula said, as pale now as she was red before. "I need your moral support. I just can't go through with it on my own."

"Come where?" Sophie said, not bothering to disguise the impatience in her voice.

"Paula invited me to accompany her to a bridge

retreat in the Hill Country," Marylou said, "and I thought you and Emma might like to join us. I thought it would be restful to be out of the city and its heat and noise for a week, and this sounded absolutely perfect. I had no idea there was another side to the plan, but I suppose I should have guessed it when Paula told me that Basil will be the guest teacher for the week."

"You could still all come and have a wonderful time," Paula said. "I just know you could. As long as you're there, I can draw courage from your presence. Being with you gives me strength, Marylou. It always has. You know that."

Marylou sighed as she got up from the table and began collecting the empty soup bowls. "I don't know, Paula. I really don't. I want some rest and relaxation, and I want to play a lot of bridge. Will you promise me that I can have all that if I come with you?"

Paula's head bobbed up and down so fast I thought she might hurt herself. "Oh, definitely, definitely," she said at last. "You'll love having Basil as a teacher—he's so patient and thoughtful. And thank the Lord, Avery won't be anywhere *near* the place!" She turned to me. "Emma, do say you'll come, too. It's a wonderful old hotel in the Hill Country where they often hold bridge retreats." She turned to Sophie. "It's really beautiful there, and I know, Sophie, that you'd all have such a lovely time. You can take lessons with Basil."

Sophie and I stared at each other across the table. I shrugged slightly, and Sophie shrugged back at me. We had both been complaining about the heat lately. This was the time of the year that Baxter and I had usually vacationed somewhere cool, and I would certainly enjoy playing bridge and learning from a master teacher, as Basil Dumont apparently was.

"I'll go," Sophie said. I echoed her words.

Paula's triumphant smile made me a bit uneasy for some reason, and I suddenly flashed on that bit of conversation Sophie and I overheard when we first arrived. She must have been talking about her current husband, Avery Trowbridge.

I relaxed. If Avery wasn't going to be at the bridge retreat, there was no point in worrying over whether Paula would make good on her threat. The worst thing we would have to endure was the woman's unceasing self-absorption.

Unfortunately, I couldn't have been more wrong.

Chapter 3

Three days later we were on our way to the Texas Hill Country.

"How much farther is it?" Sophie asked us. "I can't wait to get off the road and out of this rain."

Marylou consulted her map as I kept my hands tight on the steering wheel. The rain, though not too heavy, made me nervous, particularly since I was driving on unfamiliar roads.

"Maybe twenty minutes," Marylou said. "We turn off the highway when we get near Fredericksburg, and then it's only about ten miles down the road."

"Good," Sophie said. "I'm ready to get out of this car."

I heartily agreed with her, and I'm sure Marylou did, too. We had been on the road since about six o'clock that morning, and it was now almost quarter past ten. Had it not been for the rain that had bedeviled us for the past hour, we would probably have been there already. Mindful of the accident that had taken my husband's life, however, I wasn't about to take any chances by speeding on wet roads.

"The turnoff is just ahead," Marylou advised me. "Take the next exit, and then turn right when you get to the road. After that, according to Paula's instructions, we should be there in a few minutes."

About five minutes later, I turned the car off the highway and followed Marylou's directions. The rain persisted, and the day around us was gloomy. My husband and I had visited parts of the Texas Hill Country on several occasions, usually in the spring when the wildflowers were in bloom. The sight of roadsides, hillsides, and meadows bursting with bluebonnets and Indian paintbrush—my particular favorites—as well as other varieties, was spectacular. At the moment, however, the scenery was dreary.

To tell the truth, I was feeling a bit anxious over leaving Olaf and Hilda at home, and that anxiety no doubt colored my feelings. I had thought about bringing them along, especially when I found out that the resort where we would be staying was pet friendly. In the end, however, I decided that traveling in the car and finding themselves in a strange place would only upset them. When they were younger, Baxter and I had taken them along with us on trips, and they had adapted pretty well. They hadn't traveled in several years, though, and I thought it best to leave them at home. I had a wonderful pet sitter who actually stayed in the house with them. They liked her, and I hoped they wouldn't miss me too much.

"Stop worrying about your cats," Sophie said.

Startled, I glanced in the rearview mirror. She made a face at me, and I laughed. "You know me a little too well sometimes," I said.

"Jackie will take great care of them like she always does," Sophie said.

"I know," I said. Marylou gave my arm a little squeeze. "I promise I won't worry anymore."

"Oh, look," Marylou said, her attention diverted. She pointed. "There's the sign."

I slowed the car and prepared to turn. Ornate wrought-iron gates, connected to stone walls on either side, framed the driveway. To our left, atop the wall, sat a sign proclaiming this THE WALDHEIM HOTEL AND CONFERENCE CENTER. I drove through the open gates, and we proceeded along the driveway, following it up a gentle rise. Neatly manicured lawns dotted here and there with trees offered a prospect that was no doubt more inviting when the sun was shining.

When we reached the top of the small hill, we could see the hotel about fifty yards ahead and slightly down. I braked for a moment so we could all take in the view. The Waldheim Hotel offered a rather peculiar sight, and I peered through the rain-spattered windshield to be sure I wasn't dreaming.

What appeared to be the main part of the building resembled an antebellum mansion in the Greek Revival style, but the resemblance ended once the eyes scanned left or right. The best adjective I could come up with to describe the rest of the hotel was "haphazard." To the right of the main building, a long wing had been added at some point, and little attempt had been made to harmonize the architecture with the Greek Revival original. Perhaps whoever had built this wing had delusions of medieval grandeur, because there was a turret at the end.

The left wing gave the impression of an arm held back at a forty-five degree angle. I swung my gaze farther to the left, and there I saw the reason that the left wing was so oddly canted. The terrain sloped sharply uphill about fifty yards from the left side of the hotel, and perhaps the builder of this wing had decided it was cheaper to build sideways than to level the hill. Whatever the reason, it gave the whole building a lopsided appearance. At least it had a turret to match the other wing, providing a bit of symmetry.

"Rather odd-looking," Marylou said.

"Let's just hope it's comfortable inside," Sophie said.

"Exactly," I agreed, putting my foot to the accelerator again. I drove on to the front door of the hotel, and as I pulled to a stop, a man stepped forward with a large umbrella. He opened Marylou's door and escorted her through the rain to the porch before coming back for Sophie.

When he came for me, I asked him about parking the car.

"I'll take care of it for you, ma'am," he said. "And I'll have your bags brought to your rooms." He was about twenty-five, tall, and muscular. He looked more than capable of dealing with the car and the luggage, and I gratefully allowed him to shepherd me to the porch.

We gave him our names, and he nodded, then went back to the car. I explained to Marylou and Sophie about our bags as we went inside.

The foyer of the hotel reminded me of some of the antebellum mansions Baxter and I had visited over the years. Lots of marble, including the floor, but much of that was covered with expensive Oriental rugs. I followed Marylou and Sophie to the reception desk, to the left of the entrance.

Behind the desk stood a mousy young woman. Her fair skin was mottled with spots, and her hair could have used a good wash. Her smile was friendly, but nervous. The name tag on her blouse proclaimed her as MONICA.

"Welcome to the Waldheim," she said, her voice

thin and high-pitched. She licked her lips a couple of times before she continued. "How may I help you?"

Marylou stepped up to the desk. "We have reservations for a suite under the name Lockridge," she said.

Monica nodded before turning to consult her computer. "Yes, ma'am," she said after tapping at the keys for a few seconds. "That would be Mrs. Marylou Lockridge of Houston, accompanied by Mrs. Sophie Parker and Mrs. Emma Diamond?"

We all nodded, then began rummaging through our purses for our credit cards. Before we left Houston that morning, Marylou had tried to insist that she pay for the lodging because she had invited us. Sophie and I would have none of that. Marylou seemed to be comfortably off, but I had a feeling this place was fairly expensive. It was too much for her to pay for all three of us, and both Sophie and I could well afford to pay our own way.

Monica stared blankly at the three credit cards we handed her. "We want to split it three ways," Sophie told her, none too patiently, after the girl failed to accept even one of the cards.

Monica licked her lips again. Then she stepped back from the computer. "I don't know how to do that," she said. At least, that was what I thought she said, because her words were so faint. I could barely make them out. She turned and disappeared through a door behind her.

Marylou, Sophie, and I stared at one another for a moment, and I wondered how long we would have to stand there before someone resolved the problem. Cold air blasted through the lobby via the air-conditioning vents, and I shivered. I wanted to go to my room and warm up.

The door behind the desk opened again, and a tall woman stepped through the doorway. "I beg your pardon, ladies," she said with an insincere smile. "I'm afraid Monica is still in training, and your request presented her with a task a little too complex for a rather feeble brain."

Monica, who had just followed the woman through the door, stopped dead in her tracks, blushing unbecomingly. "I'm sorry, Mother," she said in faltering tones. "I mean, Ms. Hinkelmeier." With that, she disappeared back through the door.

Monica's mother pretended not to have heard as she accepted our three cards and began tapping at the computer.

Marylou frowned at Ms. Hinkelmeier while Sophie and I rolled our eyes at each other. If poor Monica had to put up with this kind of criticism from her mother, it was no wonder the girl had problems. How terribly unkind to say something negative about one's daughter in front of strangers—and how unforgivable.

None of us said a word as we waited for Ms. Hinkelmeier to finish what she was doing. Soon she had something for each of us to sign and, as we did, she rather ostentatiously checked our signatures on the forms against those on our credit cards. "Thank you, ladies," she said with a fake smile plastered across her face. She returned our cards, then handed us key cards for our suite.

"Leonard will show you to your suite," she said before turning away. She disappeared through the door.

We waited a minute or so before Leonard appeared. Sophie was ready to climb over the counter and go after Ms. Hinkelmeier—I could see it in her eyes. But the muscular young man with the umbrella who had parked the car turned up then.

He smiled at us, and I think we all three relaxed. He was an attractive young man, and in contrast to Ms. Hinkelmeier, he fairly radiated charm. "If you'll follow me, ladies," he said. Turning, he headed for an area behind the grand staircase.

"You're in one of our nicest suites," he informed us as he shepherded us into the elevator. "It's on the fourth floor, and you have a wonderful view of the lawns and the woods from your windows."

"That sounds lovely," Marylou said. "I'm sure we'll enjoy that."

Leonard smiled. "If there's anything I can do for you ladies while you're here, please let me know. Anything at all. I'm here to serve you." He flexed his chest as he spoke.

Marylou beamed at him, but Sophie twitched a bit at my side. I could read her mind all too well. She had picked up on the same note of ambiguity in Leonard's voice that I had. Not to mention his flexing and the way he arched one eyebrow slightly when he said the word "serve."

I was getting some very peculiar vibes from this place. First, the obnoxious Ms. Hinkelmeier, and now the suddenly servile Leonard. Just what was going on at the Waldheim Hotel?

The elevator stopped, and the door opened. Leonard stepped out and held the door for us while we exited. He led us down the hall to the end of the corridor, and Marylou handed him her key card. With a flourish, he opened the door and stood aside for us to precede him into the room.

Whatever the oddities of the hotel's personnel—at

least the three we had met thus far—the hotel itself was beautifully furnished, judging by our suite. We had entered a living room that would not have looked out of place in any of Houston's finest residential homes. Large and well-appointed, it was welcoming and comfortable. The style reminded me of an English country house, and the large windows in the wall opposite the entrance drew me right away.

Leonard was right about the view. Even through the drizzling rain, I could see the beauty of the lawns below us and the woods beyond. The view would be spectacular when the sun came out again. It was pleasant to be in the country, and I looked forward to some long walks along the paths and trails I spotted. Sophie joined me at the window for a moment while Marylou chatted with Leonard.

Sophie and I soon rejoined the other two. Leonard gave us a quick tour, pointing out the two bathrooms and two bedrooms. One bedroom had two double beds and the other had a queen-sized bed. Sophie and I insisted we take the room with the two beds while Marylou took the other one.

"Probably just as well," Marylou laughed. "Otherwise whoever roomed with me would have to put up with my snoring."

"If you ladies will just point out which luggage belongs in which rooms, I'll take care of it for you right now," Leonard said. He gestured toward the pile of suitcases in one corner of the living room.

We each claimed our bags, and Leonard, without visible effort, carried them to our rooms. Once he had finished, he reiterated his invitation to avail ourselves of his services whenever—and whatever—we needed.

Marylou gave him a handsome tip, and he winked at her as he thanked her. Sophie and I didn't say a word, because Marylou seemed to be enjoying what I hoped was a harmless bit of flirting on Leonard's part.

"Well, ladies, what do you say we unpack and then find something to eat?" Marylou said. "I don't know about you two, but I'm starving."

"I'm getting pretty hungry, too," I said. "It won't take me long to unpack."

"Last one unpacked is a rotten egg," Sophie said, giggling, as she sprinted for our bedroom.

Laughing, Marylou and I trailed behind her.

Chapter 4

We went downstairs about twenty minutes later and quickly found the dining room. I had checked my watch before we left our rooms, and it was just now going on eleven thirty. A bit early for lunch for some folk, no doubt, but since we had left Houston so early, the three of us were more than ready for something to eat.

There were a few other early birds already seated when a hostess escorted us to a square table near one of the large windows. "Your server will be with you in a moment," the hostess informed us after handing us menus.

We sat in silence for a minute or two to scan the menu. I decided on a grilled-chicken Caesar salad, folded the menu, and placed it on the table. Marylou and Sophie were still reading their menus. Glancing around the room, I groaned inwardly. Paula Trowbridge was hovering in the doorway. The minute she spotted us, she made a beeline for our table.

"Marylou, Emma, Sophie," Paula said, her tone light and happy. "I'm so glad you're here. I was hoping you'd get here early." Without waiting for an invitation, she pulled out the vacant chair across from me and sat down. She picked up my menu. "The food here is excellent. Whatever you order, I'm sure you'll just love it."

"Hello, Paula," Marylou said. "So glad you could join us." She paused. Did I detect a note of irony in Marylou's voice? "When did you get in?"

"Last night," Paula said. "What are you going to have, Emma?"

I told her my choice, and she turned to Sophie.

"I'm going to have the regular grilled-chicken salad," Sophie responded.

That left Marylou, who sighed. "I suppose I should have a salad, too, but I want something more substantial. So I'm going to have the chicken fettuccine Alfredo. I just love Alfredo sauce."

"That sounds good to me, too," Paula said. "I think that's what I'll have."

A young woman, who brightly introduced herself as Bree, said she was ready to take our orders whenever we wanted. She didn't write anything down, simply nodded her head as we spoke in turn. Next she asked what we wanted to drink, and we all asked for iced tea. "I'll be right back with your drinks," Bree promised.

"Do you think her parents were cheese fanciers?" Sophie asked. She gave us her best mock-serious expression.

"Oh, hush," I said, trying not to laugh. "It's probably short for Brianna, or something like that."

Paula frowned. "She's a very nice girl. Her parents own this place."

"Is Ms. Hinkelmeier one of the owners?" Sophie asked. "We met her when we checked in."

Paula shook her head. "No, she's the sister of the

woman whose husband is the owner." She hesitated. "To be honest, I don't care much for Veronica Hinkelmeier."

"She wasn't the warmest person I've ever met," Marylou said, "but I'm sure she must get tired of dealing with the public."

"She's very friendly with some of the public," Paula said, her voice sharp. "*Too* friendly, if you ask me."

I glanced at Sophie. She shrugged. I faced Paula. "Which of the public is she too friendly with?"

"Men, of course," Paula said, her face marred by a nasty sneer. "You should see the way she fawns all over Avery and Basil. It's disgusting. It's like she's in heat."

"How do the men respond to her?" Sophie asked.

"How do you think?" Paula snapped at her. "They're men, aren't they? The minute some woman comes on to them, they start strutting around like bantam roosters." She fell silent for a moment. "Basil isn't as bad as Avery, at least. They both have big egos, I'll admit. But Basil doesn't think only of himself all the time."

Neither man sounded like the proverbial knight in shining armor to me, but that was Paula's lookout, not mine or anyone else's. She wouldn't be the first woman who made poor choices when it came to the men in her life. Sophie was another example. She was bright, gorgeous, and just plain wonderful, yet she had married two men who were complete heels, as it turned out. At the moment she was dating one of our neighbors, Nate McGreevey. Though I had some doubts about him, so far he had proved to be a decent and thoughtful man.

No one responded to Paula's comments on the two men, but Paula frowned. Before she could say anything else, Marylou spoke. "When do the festivities start, Paula? Are we supposed to sign in somewhere?"

Trying—unsuccessfully—not to look peeved, Paula said, "There's a reception this afternoon at six thirty. If you want to officially sign in, you can do it after three in the ballroom. There should be someone there to register you."

"Is the reception very dressy?" Sophie asked. "I didn't bring anything formal with me."

Paula snorted with laughter. "You don't need to dress up to play bridge, or talk about bridge, believe me. Everyone's pretty casual at these things, though there are some women who dress like you wouldn't believe. One of them wears her blouses cut so low you'd swear she's about to lay something on the table besides cards."

Sophie giggled at that, and I couldn't suppress a smile. The image was just too funny.

"It is pretty funny," Paula said, with a sour smile, "unless your partner happens to be a man. You think a man's going to keep his mind on his cards when he's got that to look at right in front of him?"

"I know many men would find that distracting," Marylou said, "but surely not all men are that crass."

Paula snorted again. "Most of the straight ones are, let me tell you. I've been to so many of these things, following either Basil or Avery around, I am sick to death of some of these people and the way they behave. Or maybe I should say 'misbehave.'"

Sophie quirked an eyebrow at me, and I responded in kind. Our time at this bridge retreat could turn out to be interesting in a way none of us had anticipated. The way Paula was talking, it had begun to sound like we had walked onto the set of *Peyton Place*.

"Will we be expected to play duplicate while we're here?" Sophie asked.

That was a good question. Sophie had played a little duplicate, as had Marylou, but I hadn't. Another friend of mine had been urging me to join her at the local bridge studio to play duplicate, but I had been holding back. I wasn't sure I was ready to play bridge more competitively. For me it was fun, and an entertaining social activity. I wasn't sure I wanted to worry about earning points and all the trappings that went with playing duplicate bridge. But I knew my friend Dianne well enough, and I knew sooner or later she would wear me down. She was very persuasive, besides being a wonderful bridge player.

"You won't be expected to," Paula said, "but that will certainly be an option. Retreats like this, as long as they're sanctioned by the American Contract Bridge League, are a good place to earn master points. You can take the classes, and you don't have to play duplicate. There are opportunities to play rubber bridge instead."

"That's a relief," I said, smiling. "I'm not ready for duplicate yet."

"You'll be very good at it, Emma," Marylou said, "when you're ready to start. You're a fine bridge player, and all you have to remember is that you don't have to get as deeply involved in it as other people do. I never have, and I enjoy playing duplicate occasionally."

Marylou had said as much to me before. She was probably right. I would enjoy it, and my bridge skills had improved enormously since I first started playing, not long after my husband died. More experience certainly wouldn't hurt, however, and I was looking forward to the educational sessions Paula had mentioned.

Our server, Bree, reappeared at our table with our tea, and she set a tall, cold glass down in front of each of us. Marylou added several packets of artificial sweetener to hers, as did Paula. Sophie didn't add anything to hers, but I did add one packet of sweetener.

Marylou lifted her glass in a toast, and the rest of us clinked our glasses against hers. "Here's to a lovely week of playing bridge and having a good time."

"Amen to that," Sophie said. I echoed her, but Paula simply grimaced before gulping down some of her tea.

I glanced up, and over Paula's shoulder I saw Veronica Hinkelmeier approaching our table with an odd look on her face. She came to a halt beside our table.

"Mrs. Trowbridge, I hate to trouble you at a time like this," she said, but the smirk on her face belied her words. "But there's a problem with the credit card you gave us. Would you mind coming to the office with me for a minute? I'm sure we can straighten it out very quickly."

The woman made no attempt to lower her voice, and heads turned in our direction as diners at nearby tables heard what she had said. Poor Paula blushed deep red, and I felt very sorry for her. Ms. Hinkelmeier had humiliated her in public, and she made little effort to hide her enjoyment of the scene she had made. Paula seemed unable to respond for the moment, and I was so put out with the Hinkelmeier creature that I spoke before I thought much about it.

"I'm sure that the mistake is on *your* end, Ms. Hinkelmeier," I said, letting my voice carry. "After she has finished her lunch, I'm sure Mrs. Trowbridge will be more than happy to discuss the problem with you. In the meantime you might want to go back to your duties."

I used the tone I had often employed with recalcitrant high school students, and Veronica Hinkelmeier was so taken aback by my speaking up that she stood there gaping at us.

"Good day, Ms. Hinkelmeier," I said in the same firm tone. Then I turned to Paula. "I know you told me what a wonderful place this is, Paula, but frankly, the behavior of some of the staff here leaves a lot to be desired."

Sophie and Marylou were hard-pressed not to burst out laughing by this point, and even Paula was trying not to grin. I very carefully did not look in Veronica Hinkelmeier's direction again, but I could hear her breathing next to me.

Chuckles from some of the tables nearby were apparently more than Ms. Hinkelmeier could stand. From the corner of my eye, I saw her whirl around and stalk off.

"Thank you, Emma," Paula said. "I was so embarrassed I didn't know what to say. That woman despises me, and it's mutual, of course. She's such a spiteful cow."

"You're more than welcome, Paula, but I have to apologize for butting in like that. I just found her behavior so distasteful I couldn't stop myself." I said.

By now Marylou and Sophie were openly laughing. Sophie was laughing so hard, in fact, that she had to wipe the tears from her eyes. "Oh, Emma," she said, "if only you could have seen that woman's face. I bet no one has spoken to her like that in years."

"They sure haven't." Our server, Bree, had approached the table with a large tray and a tray stand. She opened the stand, set the tray on it, and began serving our food. I was very impressed with her dexterity and said so.

"Thank you, ma'am," she said, smiling shyly at me. "And whatever you want for dessert, it's on the house." Then she winked at me. "And thanks for telling off old Hinkelpuss. I wish I had the courage to do it."

"Isn't she your aunt?" Sophie asked as Bree set her salad in front of her.

Bree sighed heavily. "Unfortunately for me. I know I shouldn't say this, but I can't stand her. And the way she treats poor Monica, it's just awful."

"Thank you, dear," Marylou said, "for such speedy, efficient service. You more than make up for your aunt's lack of manners."

Bree smiled widely at that. "May I quote you on that, ma'am?"

"You certainly may," Marylou said, laughing. "And I'll be happy to tell anyone you like to their face."

Giggling, Bree departed, tray in one hand and tray stand in the other.

We all tasted our food, and we all seemed quite happy with our choices. We ate in silence for a moment, until Marylou set down her fork.

"Now, Paula, I don't want to embarrass you further," she said. "But do you think there's really a problem with your credit card? Because if there is, I'm sure I can help you until you get it straightened out."

"Thank you," Paula said, her face reddening slightly. "But I'm sure there's no real problem. It was just that witch trying to humiliate me. I'll go talk to her, but I'm sure it was all put on."

"If there's a problem, let one of us know," I said. "But after this, I doubt she'll try to get away with anything else."

Paula shook her head. "You don't know how vindictive and nasty she can be, Emma. So you'd better watch out. She's the type to bear a grudge and do something about it."

"She doesn't worry me in the slightest. If she tries anything with me, she'll draw back a nub."

Paula laughed at that, along with Marylou and Sophie.

"Now let's forget about that woman," Sophie said, "and enjoy our food."

We managed to do that for about ten minutes before being interrupted again, this time by a tall, striking man dressed in clothes so casual and simple that I knew they had to be extremely expensive.

He strolled up to our table, his tanned face alight with what I could describe only as malice.

"Well, Paula, what are you doing with these ladies? I expected to find you in Basil's bedroom."

Paula paled suddenly, her fork dropping onto the table and then flipping onto the floor. Slowly she turned around and looked up at the man standing slightly behind her.

"Avery! What the hell are you doing here?"

Chapter 5

So this was Avery Trowbridge. I eyed him curiously—and I hoped, discreetly. He was certainly handsome, with the kind of boyish, blond, blue-eyed good looks that never seem to go out of style. He was probably in his fifties, but he looked a good ten years younger. At some point, he would no doubt run to seed, but for the moment he was holding age at bay pretty well.

The smirk on his face detracted from the otherwise favorable impression of his looks, however. Even if I hadn't already heard Paula's complaints about his treatment of her, I wouldn't have taken long to get his measure.

"Now, Paula, love, is that any way to speak to your *loving* and *devoted* husband?" Avery said with sarcasm dripping from his words. He bent to give Paula a fast buss on the lips. When he straightened, though, I could see he had spotted Sophie. His eyes widened in appreciation.

Sophie easily put the rest of us in the shade. She was every bit as blond and attractive as Avery, and they certainly would have made a striking couple. From the gleam in Avery's eyes, I figured he probably was thinking the very same thing. Sophie, however, took one look at him and assumed a supremely bored expression. He wasn't her type, and he would find that out very quickly if he tried to get anywhere with her.

"Now, Paula, love, aren't you going to introduce me to your friends?"

"You still haven't explained to me what the hell you're doing here," Paula said. She fairly spit out the words. "And what the hell did you mean by such a tasteless remark about me being in Basil's bed?"

"Tut-tut, Paula, love," Avery said, his voice soothing, as if he were talking to a balky child. "I know the way your sneaky little mind works. You wouldn't be here if Basil weren't here. You can't expect me to believe you're here just because you love to play bridge so much." He threw back his head and laughed.

"Stop being a jackass, Avery," Paula said.

Avery sobered. He leaned down, then placed one hand on Paula's shoulder. From the expression on Paula's face, he must have been squeezing it rather hard. "Now, you look here, *Mrs. Trowbridge*," he said. "You lied to me about where you were going. Did you think I was going to sit idly by and let you jump into Basil's bed the moment my back was turned?"

Paula pushed back her chair suddenly and stood up, jerking Avery's hand away from her shoulder as she did so. "What the hell do *you* care whose bed I jump into?" She kept her tone low, and I could see people at the tables near us straining to hear. "As many beds as *you* jump into, you have some nerve talking to *me* like this."

"Oh my goodness, I do believe she's jealous," Avery said. If he had spoken in such a mocking tone to me, I think I would have slapped his face. "Paula, love, I had no idea you cared so much. This puts an entirely different spin on things."

Paula snapped at last. Before Avery had time to

react, she slapped him. She slapped him so hard, in fact, that he stumbled backward into a table. Luckily for him, the table was empty, but it still made a mess when it crashed over. Avery slid to the floor with it.

Paula stalked off while Avery, clearly stunned, sat on the floor for a moment. As one of the restaurant staff rushed over, Avery got to his feet and brushed himself off. He reached into his pocket and pulled out some bills, peeling a couple off the roll, and thrust them into the hands of the staff member.

"That should cover it, I trust," Avery said, as coolly as if nothing untoward had happened.

"Yes, sir," the young man stammered.

It looked to me like Avery had given him two fifties. Considering that nothing had broken during the fall, it was more than enough to cover any damages.

"Ladies, I guess we'll have to wait until later to be properly introduced." Doffing an imaginary hat, Avery bowed, then turned and walked away.

"Quite entertaining, wouldn't you say?" Sophie said before she picked up her fork and resumed eating.

"Poor Paula," I said, shaking my head. "What a horrible man."

Marylou sighed. "Now that you've met her loving husband, I think you can begin to understand some of the reasons why Paula is the way she is now. Once upon a time she was a much happier, lighthearted person."

"Then why on earth did she leave her first husband for that schmuck?" Sophie asked. "Couldn't she see what he was like?"

Marylou shook her head. "She's always been rather naive where men are concerned." She sighed again. "Besides, I said she was happier. I didn't say she was smarter."

Sophie and I exchanged amused glances. Such a negative remark was unusual for Marylou, but I supposed the circumstances were rather unusual, after all.

Marylou frowned at us. "Now, you know I didn't mean that the way it sounded."

Sophie giggled. "Are you sure? I was about to call the waitress over and order you a bowl of milk."

"Sophie! You're terrible," Marylou said, but she couldn't help laughing. "I guess it did sound pretty catty, didn't it?" She laughed again, and Sophie and I joined in.

Once the laughter had subsided, I said, "Okay, ladies, let's finish our lunch. And let's not talk about Paula and her troubles anymore."

Marylou and Sophie nodded, and we concentrated on finishing our lunch in peace. Paula never reappeared, and I was grateful, though perhaps it was mean-spirited of me to be so. I had had enough of her and her travails to last me quite a while. I doubted, however, that the respite would last.

We had finished dessert and were on our way out of the dining room when a commotion at the reception desk caught our attention. The three of us stopped, almost as one, about fifteen feet away from the desk and simply watched the disagreement.

A very large young man—at least six four and massively built—was slamming his hand against the counter. ". . . simply outrageous. What kind of establishment is this?" His face red, he glared at Veronica Hinkelmeier, who stared defiantly back at him.

"I'll thank you not to take that tone with me, mister," she said, fairly spitting at him. "I don't care who the hell you think you are. I told you, you have to have a reservation. We're fully booked right now."

"And I told you, you stupid woman, that I do have

a reservation. Can I help it if you bloody well can't read? I suggest you consult your computer again." He shoved a piece of paper across the desk at her. "Here's my confirmation. Are you trying to tell me that this is a fake?"

Veronica slapped her hand down on the paper and pulled it toward her. As we watched in complete fascination, she scanned the document. Surely she would have to admit defeat now.

But I had underestimated her.

She looked up at the man with triumph written all over her face. "You didn't guarantee this with a credit card. That's why you don't have a reservation. It was your stupid mistake, not ours." She thrust the paper back at him. "I suggest you find a room somewhere else."

"Do you know who I am?" the man demanded.

"No, and I don't give a hoot either," Veronica said. She turned her back on him.

"My name is Haskell Crenshaw," he said. "I am Avery Trowbridge's agent and business manager. Avery will not be pleased to know that I wasn't accommodated here."

Upon hearing Avery's name, Veronica whirled around. Her face quickly suffused with red. She grabbed the confirmation notice back, stuck it on the counter by her computer, and began tapping furiously at the keys.

Crenshaw watched her, a sardonic smile on his face.

Veronica looked up from the computer. Her tone devoid of inflection, she said, "It appears we do have a room for you after all." She held out her hand.

Crenshaw, now openly smirking, reached into the pocket of his suit jacket and withdrew a wallet. Opening it, he pulled out a credit card and slapped it on the counter. Veronica picked it up and swiped it before handing it back to him.

Moments later she placed a piece of paper on the counter and handed Crenshaw a pen. He signed the paper, and Veronica gave him a key when he pushed the paper off the counter toward her.

"I'd like someone to help me with my bags," Crenshaw said, in the mildest tone we had yet heard from him.

Veronica tapped the bell. Leonard appeared a few moments later. "Please escort this person to room three-nineteen, Leonard," she said.

Leonard gave her a funny look but otherwise made no comment. He scooped up Crenshaw's two bags and said, "If you'll come with me, sir." He and Crenshaw headed for the elevator.

Veronica turned and saw us before we could move away. A very unpleasant expression flitted across her face. Judging by that look, I figured we'd be lucky not to find scorpions in our beds before long. Without a word, she turned away and disappeared through the door behind the counter.

"Curiouser and curiouser," Sophie said. "The staff in this place are really something, aren't they? With charmers like her at the front desk, it's a wonder they have any people staying here at all."

"She is very unpleasant, isn't she?" Marylou said, leading the way toward the elevator.

"She's obviously a deeply unhappy person," I said. "Either that, or she was just born nasty."

"I expect she crawled from under the rock that way," Sophie said as the elevator door opened.

"Talking about Veronica, I'll bet," Leonard said while stepping out of the elevator. His attractive face split in a large grin, he stood beside the door and extended his arm against it to keep it open for us.

"Pretend you didn't hear that," Sophie said in a playful tone as she walked into the elevator. Marylou and I stepped in quickly behind her.

"Your wish is my command, dear lady." Leonard bowed deeply, and the elevator door closed as he withdrew his arm.

Sophie giggled. "He's so cute," she said.

"Yes, he is," I said, raising an eyebrow at her. "But don't forget you have someone waiting for you back in Houston."

She stuck out her tongue at me as Marylou laughed.

"Just because I've been dating Nate doesn't mean I can't enjoy the scenery," Sophie said, in a faux-haughty tone.

"I suppose not," I said, trying not to smile. Telling Sophie not to flirt with an attractive man was like telling Niagara Falls to flow backward.

The elevator door opened on the third floor, and the three of us moved back a bit to make room for Haskell Crenshaw.

"Afternoon, ladies," he said.

He was so tall his head almost brushed the ceiling of the elevator, and the space seemed too cramped for the four of us. He really was a big man.

"Good afternoon," Marylou said politely as the doors closed.

Crenshaw glanced at the panel of buttons and nodded. Apparently his destination was also the fourth floor.

When the elevator halted and the doors opened, he stepped out and held the door open for us.

"Thank you," we chorused. We headed down the hall toward our suite, and Crenshaw trailed behind us.

We had reached our door, and Sophie inserted the key. Crenshaw knocked on the door nearest ours.

Sophie lingered with our door, appearing to have some problem with the key. I suspected, however, that she was delaying opening the door because she wanted to see who answered Crenshaw's knock.

We didn't have to wait long. The door opened, and Avery Trowbridge stepped forward.

"Haskell, what the hell are you doing here? When I fire someone, they stay fired." With that, Trowbridge slammed the door in his former agent's face.

Chapter 6

Sophie pushed our door open, and the three of us scuttled into the suite, shutting the door behind us. Marylou sank down in one of the overstuffed armchairs, and Sophie and I seated ourselves on the sofa.

Before any of us could say anything, we heard a dull pounding noise coming from the hall. Sophie got up and went to the door. Opening it slightly, she peered out. She stood there for almost a minute while the pounding continued.

The sound ceased, and Sophie watched at the door a moment longer. She closed it and came back to sit beside me on the sofa.

"What was all that about?" Marylou asked.

"That Crenshaw person was pounding on Avery Trowbridge's door," Sophie said. I had guessed as much. "Trowbridge finally opened the door and let him in the room, but from the glimpse I caught of his face, he didn't look any too happy about it."

"What on earth have we gotten ourselves into?" Marylou said, looking more than a bit perturbed. "I'm not sure I like the idea of us being in the suite next to such goings-on."

"It's nothing to do with us, really," I said. "We're

here to play bridge, and that's what we're going to do. We'll mind our own business, and we should be fine." I tried to invest as much confidence into my tone as I could. Of course I should have known better, but despite the things we had seen today, I still thought we would be able to stay out of it.

"I don't like it," Marylou said, frowning. "I wish I had never let Paula talk me into coming here. And then I talked you two into coming as well. I'm so sorry."

"There's nothing for you to apologize for," Sophie said, waving a hand in the air. "Frankly, I'm finding it all more than a bit interesting." She laughed. "This is better than watching a soap opera."

Marylou frowned at her. "It may be amusing to you, but I've got a bad feeling about all this. All these tensions, well, I'm sure something bad will happen. Just wait till Basil Dumont finds out that Avery is here. He won't like that one bit."

"Let me guess," I said. "They aren't best friends?"

"No, they're not," Marylou said. "They can't stand each other. Basil resents it because Avery's more successful than he is, and Avery thinks Basil is a pompous little twit." She sighed. "And Paula has managed to put herself right between them."

"A big, stinking mess," I said, frowning. Despite my positive words to the contrary just moments ago, I was beginning to think it might be a good idea for us to pack our bags and head for Houston.

Sophie apparently read my mind, for she turned to me and said, "Now, Emma, don't start talking about going home. It's nice to be out of Houston for a week, and I don't care what else is going on here. We're going to have fun. We'll play a lot of bridge, eat a lot of good food, and relax and enjoy ourselves."

I capitulated. "You're right, you're right. We'll stay out of the way as much as possible, and maybe they'll stay out of our way."

"Good idea," Marylou said. She yawned. "You know, I think I'll have a little nap. After all that good food and that long drive this morning, I'm a little tired." She got up from her chair. "What are you two going to do?"

Sophie got up and went to the window. "Still raining," she announced. "I really would like to go for a walk, but not in such messy weather."

"I think I'll read awhile," I said. "We really don't have anything to do this afternoon except check in with the bridge-retreat people at some point, and the reception at six thirty."

"I'm going to explore the hotel a bit. I can get my walk in that way, at least," Sophie said. "You two relax, and I'll find out where everything is."

Marylou yawned again and waved at us as she ambled off to her bedroom. She shut the door softly behind her.

"Sure you don't want to come with me, Emma?" Sophie asked as she headed for the door.

I was sorely tempted to stay in our suite and read, but curiosity got the better of me. It often did, I had to admit. "Sure, why not?" I got up and followed her out the door.

We both shot curious glances at Avery Trowbridge's door as we passed it, but everything was quiet at the moment. We proceeded down the hall to the elevator, and Sophie punched the down button.

"Where to first?" I asked. "You're the cruise director."

When the doors opened, I followed Sophie inside.

"I thought we might check out the ballroom first," Sophie said. "That's where the reception will be, and

I believe that's where we'll be playing bridge most of the time."

On the ground floor we followed the signs for the ballroom, and the closer we came to it, the more noise we could hear.

The doors were open, and Sophie and I paused on the threshold. Before us we could see the proverbial beehive of activity in a space large enough to hold a couple of hundred people very easily. Several men were setting up tables and chairs, while other men covered the tables with tablecloths. Two women followed behind them, setting out attractive flower arrangements, along with some sort of party favors. Against the wall at the center of the long room, three people were preparing the dais for the reception. We wandered into the room, out of the way of the workers. They paid us no attention.

Lightning flashed, drawing our attention to the French doors along the outside wall. Placed every six feet or so, they were separated by large windows that extended from about my knee level up to within five feet of the high ceiling. I closed my eyes for a moment, imagining this space in the spring, on a lovely late afternoon. A tea perhaps, or a wedding reception. Maybe a fiftieth wedding anniversary.

I grimaced. Thinking of wedding anniversaries was like worrying a sore tooth—painful and unproductive.

Sophie prodded me in the side, then indicated with a sideways bob of her head that I should look back at the doorway to the ballroom about six feet away.

Veronica Hinkelmeier had just walked in, accompanied by a tall, rail-thin man clutching a clipboard to his chest. He was sixtyish, with sparse gray hair and oversized glasses that gave him the look of a confused owl. He blinked at us, while Veronica simply scowled.

"As you can see, Mr. Dumont," Veronica said, "preparations are well in hand. Everything will be ready in plenty of time."

So this was Basil Dumont. I eyed him with more curiosity. His clothes were well made but beginning to show their age. The seat of his pants was shiny, and the elbows of his shirt appeared to be fraying a bit.

Avery Trowbridge, jerk though he seemed to be, definitely had the edge when it came to looks and grooming, but perhaps Basil Dumont compensated by having a far more likable personality. At the moment, though, I was hard-pressed to figure out what Paula saw in either of them.

When he spoke, Dumont's voice was a surprise. Instead of the reedy tenor I expected, he possessed the rich baritone of an opera singer. Sophie twitched beside me as we both responded to the sound.

"I'm sure you're right, Veronica," he said, "but you know I like to check on these things myself." He flourished his clipboard. "Don't let me detain you. I know you have many things to attend to."

Veronica's eyebrows arched in annoyance, but she didn't argue. Turning on her heel, she stalked off.

Basil Dumont uttered something under his breath, something that sounded suspiciously like "harpy." Sophie and I exchanged glances, smiling. Then Dumont caught sight of us, and his expression became guarded.

"Good afternoon, Mr. Dumont," Sophie said, stepping forward and extending a hand. "I can't tell you what a pleasure it is to meet you at last. I've read several of your books, and I recommend them to anyone who wants to learn more about bridge."

Like any straight male not on his deathbed, Dumont responded quickly to Sophie. His eyes lingered for a moment over her exquisite figure before he accepted her hand. He sketched a very courtly bow over it. "My pleasure, ma'am."

Sophie giggled, and Dumont beamed. Three minutes more of this, and he would be thoroughly besotted. I hid a smile.

"I'm Emma Diamond," I said, extending my own hand. "And this is Sophie Parker."

Dumont offered me the same courtesy of a bow, but I would have sworn he never took his eyes off Sophie.

"It's a pleasure to meet two such charming ladies," he said, straightening and letting go of my hand. "I take it you're both here for the bridge retreat?"

As we both assented, he said, "How delightful! I shall look forward to working with you."

I turned my head away so that I wouldn't laugh in his face. He still hadn't taken his eyes off Sophie. I was so used to this reaction, I simply found it amusing.

Sophie giggled again, and Dumont was almost licking his lips. What he didn't know, of course, was that Sophie always found these situations as funny as I did.

I had asked her once why she egged men on this way, and she just laughed. "Because they enjoy it, Emma, and so do I. It's pretty harmless."

"Basil!"

Until she shrieked out the poor man's name, none of us had noticed Paula Trowbridge approaching. I might have imagined it, but I would have sworn that Dumont winced at the sound of his former wife's voice. His shoulders did tense slightly, and they stayed that way for several minutes.

When he turned to greet Paula, however, he had a pleasant smile on his face. Sophie and I watched the reunion with interest. As far as I could tell, Paula hadn't registered the fact that Sophie and I were standing right there.

"Paula, my dear, what a pleasant surprise," Basil said. His tone lacked warmth, but at least it wasn't outright rude.

He held out his hand to her. Paula, about to launch herself into his arms, halted awkwardly and stood staring at the outstretched hand. She took his hand with a woebegone look on her face. After a moment's pause, she clasped the hand to her bosom and stared soulfully up into Dumont's eyes.

"Basil. I can't *tell* you how I have longed for this moment, to be reunited with you."

I swear that's what she said. I couldn't have made up more clichéd dialogue if I had tried.

Dumont tried to free his hand, but Paula had an iron lock on it. He tugged, feebly at first, then with increasing strength, and finally she let go.

Shaking his hand, as if to restore the circulation, Dumont gave Paula a pained smile.

"It's nice to see you, Paula, dear," Dumont said, "but I really do have to get to work. You'll have to excuse me. Perhaps we can chat later." He turned away.

Sophie and I should have slipped by them and disappeared before now, because our presence made things very awkward for Paula. She had finally noticed us, and her cheeks reddened in embarrassment.

"Yes, Basil, dear, I'm sure you must have so much to do, but you know if there's anything I can do to assist you, all you have to do is ask."

By now, Dumont had moved well away from us, and I doubted whether he had even heard her.

"Sophie, Emma," Paula said, "what are you two doing

here?" She glared at us as if she had caught us stealing something from her purse.

"Just exploring the hotel," Sophie said. "We wanted to find out where everything is."

"Yes," I said, "it's such a large place, and it really is lovely inside, don't you think? The ballroom in particular."

Paula nodded curtly. "I'll see you later. I've got things to do." She stalked off.

"There goes Miss Charm School of 1966," Sophie said, low enough so that only I could hear.

I suppressed a laugh. "You're incorrigible."

"Just one of the many reasons I'm your best friend," she said, tossing her head. "Come on. We've got more exploring to do. I want to find out where the gym is, and if they have an indoor pool."

We could have gone back to our suite and consulted the hotel guide there, but Sophie headed for the reception desk instead. Trailing in her wake, I hoped we would be lucky enough to find someone besides Veronica Hinkelmeier staffing the desk.

No such luck. Not only was Veronica at the desk, glaring at a woman and a young man standing in front of it, but Paula was there, too.

"Lorraine, what are you doing here?" we heard Paula ask. She stood a few feet away from the woman and the young man, her back rigid.

Sophie and I glanced at each other. What now?

The woman Paula had addressed, an attractive red-head in her late forties, turned slowly and faced Paula. "Oh, goody, just what I needed to make this joyful day complete. One stupid bitch behind the desk, and the queen of them all here to greet me."

Chapter 7

"Mom!" The young man, with hair a paler version of his mother's fiery mane, put a hand on her arm. "Not now."

"Relax, Will," she said. Her gaze softened when she looked at her son. When she focused on Paula again, however, her eyes hardened.

"Just stay out of my way, Paula, and you won't get hurt," she said. Then, turning her back on Paula, she faced Veronica again. "I have a reservation, and you'd better stop stalling and let us have our rooms. I'm sure you wouldn't want me to discuss your customer relations with your boss. I don't think he would be happy to know just how *hospitable* you are to other women's husbands."

Obviously furious, Veronica stood and stared across the counter at the woman who now smiled serenely back at her. Taking a deep breath, Veronica began fiddling with her computer.

Paula, with an obvious lack of common sense, moved closer to the redhead. "Now, listen, Lorraine. Everything's going to be fine. Really, it will be. I've asked Avery for a divorce, and you can have him back."

So Lorraine was the former Mrs. Trowbridge, the one whom Avery had divorced in order to marry Paula. I glanced at Sophie—she was intent on the scene before us. We really should have left at that point, but we were both far too curious to do so.

Lorraine Trowbridge motioned for her son to sign the paper Veronica had thrust across the counter. With a fierce frown, he did so. A sardonic smile on her lovely face, Lorraine moved closer to Paula.

"Why on earth would I want Avery back now? I wouldn't touch him with a ten-foot pole after he's been with you."

"I don't want him either," Paula said, her shoulders tensing. "He's a bastard, and I just want to be free of him."

"My, my," Lorraine said. "And after you worked so hard to get him. All that time on your back, and now you don't want him anymore." She turned toward the counter. "Did you hear that, Veronica? Paula doesn't want him anymore, so now's your chance. You might as well put all the time *you* spent on *your* back to good use. Avery is obviously up for grabs."

"Mom, come on," Will Trowbridge said. He was patently embarrassed by what had transpired. He picked up their luggage, two large bags, and started moving in the direction of the elevator. "Come on, Mother, now, please."

Yielding to her son, Lorraine followed him and the luggage, but not before casting one last nasty, triumphant smile at Paula and Veronica.

Veronica stalked into the office behind the desk and slammed the door. Paula turned in our direction, and she wilted even further right before our eyes.

"I've made such a mess of things," she said, in the most woebegone voice I'd ever heard. Since that was so obviously true, neither Sophie nor I had a response. I did feel sorry for her, though, so I moved closer to her and slipped an arm around her shoulders.

"Why don't you go to your room and rest," I said. "You've had a rough few hours, and I think a good nap will make you feel better."

"Exactly," Sophie said, patting Paula's arm. "Listen to Emma. Go take a long hot bath to relax, and then have a nap."

"Thank you," Paula said, her lower lip trembling. "I think I will." Sobbing softly to herself she turned away from us and went toward the elevator.

Sophie and I waited until the elevator had come and carried Paula away before we moved. Sophie turned to me. "This is some little soap opera."

"No kidding," I said, shaking my head. "And I have a nasty feeling it's just going to get a lot worse before we're done with it." I headed for the elevator. "Come on, I don't know about you, but I'm ready for a little quiet time." I punched the call button.

Sophie shook her head. "No, you go ahead. I still want to check out the gym. I really ought to put in some time on a treadmill today if I can."

I laughed. "You and your treadmill. Oh, well, have fun. I'm going upstairs." The elevator doors opened, and I stepped inside.

"See you later," Sophie said as the doors shut.

Back in our suite, everything was quiet. Marylou must still be napping, I thought, and moved with care through the living room area to the bedroom I was sharing with Sophie. I pulled off my shoes, retrieved my book from my bag, and made myself comfortable on the bed.

As I read, I could feel my eyelids drooping, and after a few minutes, I surrendered to the drowsiness and put the book aside. I closed my eyes, nestling down in the bed, and before long I dropped off.

I awoke sometime later when Sophie slipped into the room. Yawning, I sat up.

"Sorry if I woke you," she said. "When I came in earlier, you were sound asleep." She wore her exercise togs, but from what I could see, she didn't appear to have broken a sweat.

"No, I need to get up and start stirring around." I moved to the side of the bed and put my feet on the floor. Yawning again, I glanced at my watch. "Good grief, it's almost five thirty."

"And the reception starts at six thirty," Sophie said. "If you don't mind, I'm going to hop in the shower to freshen up. I won't be long."

"Go right ahead," I said, yawning again. "I need to wake up a little, and then I probably should take a quick shower myself."

Sophie disappeared into the bathroom, and I got up from the bed and wandered out into the living room. I walked over to Marylou's door, which stood slightly ajar, and knocked.

When I received no answer, I pushed the door open and took a step inside. "Marylou," I called. I listened for sounds of movement from her bathroom, but all was quiet. She wasn't in the suite. I went back to the living room and paced around a bit to wake myself up completely.

I was on my fourth circuit of the room when I heard the door from the hall opening.

Marylou came in, and from the look on her face, I could tell something was wrong.

"Are you okay?" I asked, moving toward her. "You look like you want to murder someone."

Marylou pushed the door shut behind her, then

leaned against it. "I'll give you three guesses, and the first two don't count."

"Paula?"

She nodded. "Of course. I was sound asleep, enjoying a nice nap, when the phone rang. It was Paula."

"I didn't even hear the phone," I said.

"It rang only once," Marylou said. "I wake very quickly, and I picked it up before it could ring again."

"Come on over here and sit down a minute," I said, heading for the sofa. Marylou followed me and plopped down beside me. "So what was it this time?"

"More of the same," Marylou said, shaking her head tiredly. "I gather you and Sophie were on the scene when Paula ran into Lorraine Trowbridge and her son."

I nodded. "Another unpleasant little encounter."

"Well, Paula wanted a shoulder to cry on," Marylou said, "and I obliged." She sighed. "If this goes on much longer, my shoulders will start to mildew."

I laughed, and Marylou smiled. It was a rather grim smile, however. "You're a good friend to put up with her."

"I suppose," Marylou said. "She's just so gosh-darned pathetic right now, and I can't find it in my heart to turn her away when she needs to talk to somebody. I suppose I'm helping her, but no matter what I say, I'm not sure she really hears what I'm telling her."

"Just look at it this way," I said. "You're shortening your time in purgatory in a big way."

She laughed outright at that, and I was pleased to see her normally cheerful demeanor returning.

"Where's Sophie?" she asked.

"In the shower," I said. "I need to take a quick one myself, so I can get ready for the reception."

"Oh, good grief," Marylou said, forcing herself up from the sofa. "I completely forgot about that dad-blamed reception. I need a shower, too." She frowned. "It's at six thirty, isn't it?"

"Yes," I said, glancing at the clock on the wall. "That gives us about forty-five minutes to get ready."

Marylou relaxed a bit. "Plenty of time, then. But I guess I'll go ahead and have a shower." She disappeared into her bedroom and shut the door.

I got up from the sofa and wandered back into my bedroom. Sophie had finished her shower and was sitting at the dressing table doing her makeup. "Shower's all yours," she said.

"Thanks." I gathered my things and busied myself in the bathroom.

At a few minutes past six thirty, the three of us were ready for the reception. Sophie wore cream slacks and a stunning blue silk blouse that set off her blond hair and tanned skin to perfection, while Marylou had chosen an emerald pantsuit with a white shell. I had opted for my favorite red silk top and black slacks, accompanied by a wide red, white, and black belt. The belt was very 1960s, but I loved it. Sophie grinned when she saw it.

"That's so retro," she said, "but on you, it actually works."

"Thank you," I said. "I think."

"We all look very nice," Marylou said. "Casual but elegant." She beamed at us as proudly as if we were her daughters.

After Sophie and I gave her a quick hug, we were out the door and on the way to the reception. Sixty to seventy people milled about in the ballroom, and a few more entered behind the three of us. The transformation of the room was complete. If anyone had wondered what the theme of this party was, the decorations ought to be a big clue. Large playing cards hung from the ceiling at intervals, and I counted them. There were thirteen—in other words, a bridge hand.

Quite a hand it was, too, I decided as I assessed the cards. Twenty-seven high card points—almost enough for a slam bid in one hand.

I examined the rest of the room. Suspended over the dais were two large bridge scorepads, partially filled in. I moved on to the tables. Each of them sported a flower arrangement, and looming out of each arrangement were large cards, continuing the pattern of the large cards overhead.

I realized with a start that Marylou and Sophie had left me to goggle at the room on my own. I spotted them near the buffet table and walked over to them, wending my way through the milling crowd.

"Look at this spread," Sophie said. She held a small plate, empty at the moment. "Too many choices."

I agreed as I looked over the long table. There were platters of crudités with dip in the center, plates of delicious-looking cheeses with bread and crackers, a mound of grapes and sliced apples on a tray, and a selection of meats and breads for small sandwiches. A table nearby held a tempting array of dessert items, like miniature cheesecakes, pecan pies, and éclairs, just to name a few.

The three of us made our choices before going to the bar for drinks. Then, drinks in hand, we found an unoccupied table and sat down. There were eight places at each table, and before long our table filled up. We introduced ourselves to the newcomers, one of whom was a twelve-year-old girl attending with her grandmother.

The grandmother proudly informed us that the young

girl was a whiz at bridge and had already accumulated an impressive number of points toward being named a Life Master. The girl, whose name was Alice McCarthy, blushed and tried, without success, to restrain her grandmother, Lucinda McCarthy. Before too many minutes had elapsed, everyone at our table knew more than any of us could ever wish to know about Alice's prowess, while Alice hunched so far down in her chair I thought she would soon disappear under the table.

Taking pity on the poor girl, I engaged her in conversation, and Marylou did her best with the grandmother. We had made some headway when we were all startled by a voice booming out across the room. We all turned toward the dais to see a beaming Basil Dumont at the podium.

"Thank you for your attention, ladies and gentlemen," he said. He paused for a long moment to let the residual chatter die down. "We're all so pleased you could join us for this wonderful event here at this beautiful hotel. Isn't the hotel doing a great job for us?"

Again he paused, this time for some rather lukewarm applause from the audience.

Sophie leaned toward me. "I guess most of them have met Veronica Hinkelmeier, too, and they don't like her any more than we do." She kept her voice low, but people nearby heard her.

One man guffawed, then said, "You got that right, honey." He winked at Sophie, who smiled back at him.

Alice had heard her as well. Her face solemn, she regarded me. "That's the lady that checked us in, isn't she?"

I nodded.

Alice frowned. "She was really rude to Nana and

me when we checked in. I thought she was just having a bad day, but I guess she did it to other people, too."

"I think for her, Alice, every day must be a bad day," I said, and Alice giggled.

Basil Dumont's voice boomed out again. He launched into a lengthy description of the week's activities. The only important thing he said, as far as I was concerned, was that play would begin promptly at seven thirty. That pleased me. I was itching to play some bridge and forget about all the unpleasantness I had witnessed today.

Dumont had neared the end of his remarks when I noticed someone approaching the dais from the side. Avery Trowbridge slowly climbed the steps and came to a halt about three feet away from Dumont, so far still oblivious to the other man's presence. Dumont thanked the audience and began to turn away, in the direction of Trowbridge.

"What the hell are you doing up here?" Dumont said. When he realized that everyone in the room had heard him, he flushed dark red.

Trowbridge didn't speak to him. He stepped around his erstwhile rival to reach the microphone. Dumont stood helplessly by, sputtering incoherently.

"Good evening, everyone," Avery Trowbridge said. "I just wanted to let you all know that you have an alternative here during the coming week. I'll be available for private instruction, and also as a partner for those wishing to earn some master points." He flashed a cocky grin. "I have a card with my fees, and I'll be happy to talk to you." He waved and turned away.

He made the mistake of turning his back to Basil Dumont. Obviously enraged by Trowbridge's announcement, Dumont took a wild swing at the back of Trowbridge's head. The blow missed his head, but it connected with his shoulder, hard enough to knock Trowbridge off his feet.

Trowbridge scrambled to right himself, clutching at the table next to him on the dais, but he couldn't. With a resounding crash, he and the table went off the dais and onto the floor.

Chapter 8

Everyone sat in stunned silence as Avery Trowbridge made contact with the floor, landing with the table beneath him. We were sitting too far away to be of practical use, but several people sitting much closer quickly got to their feet to check on Avery.

I shot a glance at the dais. Basil Dumont stood unmoving, an odd expression on his face. Remorse? Triumph? Satisfaction? I couldn't decide. I was surprised at how violent his attack on Avery had been.

By now two men had helped Avery Trowbridge to his feet, and he appeared not to have suffered any serious injury from the fall. He dusted himself off, thanking the men who had come to his aid.

"Avery!" A shrill voice cut through the hubbub surrounding the accident victim, and for a moment I thought it was Paula who had spoken.

Veronica Hinkelmeier pushed her way through the people now milling about. A couple of hotel employees had stepped forward to remove the table and clean up the debris from the fall. Trowbridge had turned to scowl at Basil Dumont when he was nearly knocked off his feet again by Veronica's onslaught. She threw her arms around him, oblivious to the stares of those nearby.

"Avery, darling, are you all right?"

Avery Trowbridge thrust her away from him, almost violently, and Veronica stumbled, nearly falling herself.

"I'll thank you to keep your hands off me," Avery said, and the chill in his voice was palpable, and his voice rang through the room. Everyone had to have heard him.

Veronica Hinkelmeier blinked at him, obviously stunned by his reaction. Trowbridge turned away from her, fixing upon Basil Dumont, still standing on the dais. "Look here, Dumont," he said.

That was all he managed to get out before Veronica launched herself at him. Her fist connected with the back of his head, and he stumbled against the dais.

"You bastard! How dare you treat me like that!" She stood there, her chest heaving. "I wish you were dead."

Trowbridge turned back to face her. As he rubbed the back of his head with one hand, he smirked at her. "Funny, you took the words right out of my mouth, you stupid cow."

Leonard, the attractive young man who seemed to be a combination of concierge and bellboy, stepped through the crowd to maneuver himself between Veronica and Trowbridge. He spoke quietly, and we were far enough away that I couldn't hear anything of what he said. It apparently was effective, whatever he said, because Veronica allowed him to lead her from the room.

Trowbridge was left standing there, looking faintly ridiculous. The buzz of conversation had resumed, and I wondered how on earth anyone could settle down to playing bridge after this little tempest.

Basil Dumont seemed to have recovered his composure as he spoke into the microphone again. "Ladies and gentlemen," he said, his voice quavering only slightly, "in just a few minutes the hotel staff will be setting up screens to partition the ballroom for our bridge playing. Roughly two-thirds of the ballroom will be dedicated to those playing duplicate, and the other third for those who don't wish to play duplicate. Please enjoy your food, and I'll be back soon to get you started playing bridge."

As he exited the dais, conversations resumed around the room. I watched him for a moment before he disappeared through a door at the back of the ballroom. Avery Trowbridge made no move to follow him, which rather surprised me. Perhaps, though, Trowbridge had had enough confrontation for the moment. Still rubbing the back of his head, he moved over to the food tables and began filling a plate.

"That was surely something to see," Marylou said in a low voice.

"No kidding," Sophie said. "Welcome to the circus, ladies."

"Where is Paula?" I asked, suddenly realizing that I hadn't seen her since we had entered the ballroom.

"She was going to have a nap and join the festivities later," Marylou said. "And it's just as well, given what happened here. No telling what she might have done."

"Can you believe that Hinkelmeier woman?" Sophie asked, leaning closer to me. "I mean, she might as well have announced to everyone in the room that she's in love with the man."

"He certainly doesn't appear to feel the same way about her," I said, doing my best not to sound catty.

"Amen to that," Marylou said.

Alice and her grandmother were watching us, and

I mustered up a smile. "Very strange goings-on," I said with a polite smile.

Her head bobbing up and down, Alice giggled. Her grandmother sniffed loudly. "I have a good mind to take Alice home first thing tomorrow morning. I'm not sure I want my precious granddaughter exposed to such vulgar scenes."

Frankly, I couldn't blame the woman, but Alice evidently had other ideas. She turned to her grandmother with a pouting face. "But I don't want to go home, Nana. You promised!"

Nana's stern face softened. "All right, dear," she said. "We'll stay so you can play. But I want you to stay away from those people as much as possible."

"Of course, Nana," Alice said with a prim smile. Her eyes cut to me with a sly look, and it was all I could do not to laugh. Nana was outmatched—that much I knew.

"I'm going back for dessert," Marylou said, standing up, plate in hand. "Emma, Sophie?"

I glanced down at my empty plate. I really shouldn't, but I remembered those miniature cheesecakes. Cheesecake was one of my weak points, where willpower usually failed me. Sighing, I pushed my chair back and stood up. Why break a perfect record?

Picking up my plate, I followed Marylou to the food tables. Sophie remained behind, chatting with Alice and her grandmother. Marylou and I joined the short line at the buffet, and I gazed curiously about.

Avery Trowbridge sat at a table just a few feet away. Several of the seats at the table were occupied, but it didn't appear that any of the people at the table wished to converse with Trowbridge. He ate slowly and steadily, looking neither left nor right, staring straight ahead.

For a moment, our gazes locked, and Trowbridge quirked one eyebrow. I stared blandly back at him before turning away. A moment later I sneaked a peek at him, and he had gone back to staring into space as he ate.

The line moved forward, and I reached for a cheese-cake, hesitating for a moment between chocolate swirl and plain. I went for the plain—why compound my lapse any further? In the meantime Marylou had put two cheesecakes and one éclair on her plate. I grinned, and Marylou saw me.

"One of the cheesecakes is for Sophie," she told me, her tone slightly defensive.

I nodded, repressing my amusement.

As we turned to go back to our table, I noticed a woman who had been ahead of Marylou in line. With a start, I recognized her as Lorraine Trowbridge. She held a heaping plate of dip with a few pieces of raw vegetables, and I watched in horrified fascination as she approached her ex-husband. I poked Marylou in the side, and she stopped to watch, too.

Trowbridge glanced up to see his ex-wife approaching. His mouth twisted in an expression of distaste. "Lorraine, what the hell are you doing here? Is Will with you?"

"Hello, Avery," Lorraine said, coming to a halt very close to Trowbridge. "Yes, your son is here. Frankly I'm amazed that you even remember that you have a son. In case you've forgotten, he's the one who has been waiting on money from you so he can pay his tuition for this semester."

Trowbridge started to rise from his chair. "Now, look, Lorraine, I told you, my so-called manager has screwed up my finances, and I don't have the money right now."

"Oh, give it a rest, Avery," Lorraine said. "Every time Will has needed something from you, it's the same old excuse. I'm really rather tired of hearing it, because I know better. I know your little game. You're a cheap bastard who can't be bothered to support his only child, and you know it."

Trowbridge opened his mouth to speak, but before he could get the first syllable out, Lorraine threw her plate at him. Upon impact, Trowbridge sank with a thump into his chair.

Lorraine leaned down and said, "That's the nicest thing that's going to happen to you, you bastard. If you don't come across with that money by tomorrow, I'm going to rip your balls off and feed them to you. Do you understand me?"

Trowbridge nodded, even as he was wiping the dip from his eyes.

"Good," Lorraine said. She walked off.

Marylou and I scurried back to our table then.

"What was going on over there?" Sophie asked us as we sat down. Alice McCarthy and her grandmother had departed. We had the table to ourselves.

I filled her in, and she laughed. "Serves the jerk right," Sophie said when I had finished. "Lorraine sounds like one tough broad."

"I certainly wouldn't want to get on her bad side," I responded. I watched Marylou put a piece of cheesecake on Sophie's plate. "I just can't believe he sat there and took it, though. He actually acted like he was intimidated by her."

"Well, she threatened him, didn't she?" Marylou said. "Didn't you hear that one thing she told him?" She forked a piece of cheesecake into her mouth.

The light dawned then. "'I know your little game,'" I quoted.

"Exactly," Marylou said.

"What do you think she meant?" Sophie asked. She played with her own piece of cheesecake, taking tiny bites of it.

"It's only a theory, mind you," Marylou said, laying her fork aside for the moment. "But I'd be willing to bet you that Avery and his accountant are in trouble with the IRS. He said his manager had screwed up his finances, right?"

I nodded.

"It sounds to me like they were trying to cheat the IRS, and they got caught," Marylou said triumphantly. She picked up her fork and ate the rest of her cheesecake.

"That's certainly plausible," I said. "Avery does seem like the type. I wouldn't trust him for a minute."

"My money's on Lorraine, though," Sophie said. "She'll get what she wants, and to hell with Avery."

Marylou and I agreed.

I looked over toward the table where Avery had been sitting, and he was no longer there. He had gone somewhere to clean up, no doubt. I wondered whether he would turn up again tonight. After all that had happened, I wouldn't have the nerve to show my face again if I were with him, but somehow I figured that none of this would faze Avery enough to keep him in his room.

I was proved right about half an hour later when Basil Dumont returned to get the play started. He stood once again on the dais, to give out instructions. As everyone moved about to his or her chosen side of the divided room, I saw Avery Trowbridge slip back into the ballroom. He sidled into our area of the room, perhaps because Basil Dumont was busy in the section reserved for duplicate bridge. Avery held some papers in his hands, and he began going from table to table, stopping briefly at each one. Occasionally he wrote something down on one of the pages before moving on to the next table.

Marylou had elected to play duplicate this week, but Sophie and I had firmly resisted any suggestions that we join her. I wasn't ready for the pressure of duplicate, and Sophie just plain didn't want to work that hard, though she was more than skilled enough to be an excellent duplicate player. The other two players at our table were two men from Galveston named Bob and Bart, retired schoolteachers, as we discovered. They had taken up bridge in retirement as a way to keep their minds active.

I had dealt the first hand and was getting ready to bid when Avery Trowbridge finally made his way to our table. "Good evening, ladies, gentlemen," he said, his voice smooth. "Pardon me for interrupting. I'll only take a moment of your time." He paused to see that he had our attention.

Flourishing the sheets of paper in his hand, he explained. "I'm offering half-hour sessions with me, beginning at nine tomorrow morning. Three people at a time. I'm even offering a steep discount this week, so now's your chance. Anyone here interested?"

Bob raised his hand as he glanced at his companion. "We are." Bart nodded.

Smiling, Avery asked them both their names and room numbers. When Bart gave him the same room number, Avery smirked for a moment, but he scribbled something on his paper. "I've got you two down for nine. That leaves one more slot for that half hour. Ladies?" He looked from Sophie to me and back again.

Sophie shook her head, and I was about to do the

same. Then I changed my mind. Put it down to nothing more than blatant curiosity about the man. I wanted to see if he acted like a human being when he was teaching. He had to have earned his reputation in the bridge world somehow.

"Yes," I said. "Put me down for nine also." I looked at Bart and Bob. "You don't mind?"

"Of course not," they chorused.

"Thanks," I said before giving Avery my name and room number.

"Right," Avery said. "I'll see you at nine tomorrow morning in my suite." He gave the room number before going on to the next table.

"Should be interesting," I said.

Bob laughed. "After everything that's been happening, I can't wait to see what's going to happen next."

Sophie and Bart laughed along with him. I had to smile, but inside I felt troubled. I had bad feelings about everything I had witnessed today, and I was afraid there was worse to come tomorrow.

As it turned out, I was right.

Chapter 9

By nine thirty both Sophie and I were feeling pretty tired, so we made our excuses to Bob and Bart. The men brushed aside our apologies.

"Don't give it another thought," Bob said. "We've been to this event before. There will be plenty of people to play with till probably two or three in the morning." He smiled at us. "You go and rest, and we'll see you tomorrow."

Sophie and I beat a rapid retreat to our suite. Marylou was nowhere to be seen. I called out her name but got no response.

"She had that nap this afternoon, remember," Sophie said, suppressing a yawn as she preceded me into our bedroom. "I'm going to brush my teeth and change. Mind if I hog the bathroom for a few minutes?"

"Go for it," I told her, while sinking gratefully down on the bed. I slipped off my shoes and flopped backward, with my legs hanging off the end of the bed. The mattress felt comfortable, and I thought with a pang of my cats, Olaf and Hilda. This was my first night without them in quite some time, and I would miss their comforting presence on the bed with me. I knew they would be missing me, too, because they hated any disruption of their routine. I pictured them roaming around the house, looking for me. "Oh, stop it," I told myself. "They'll be okay. It's just for a few days, and you know Jackie will take good care of them."

"Talking to yourself already," Sophie said, laughing at me a little. I hadn't heard her come back into the room. "Really, Emma, stop worrying about your cats." She had a live-in housekeeper to look after her dogs, but unfortunately the woman was afraid of cats. Otherwise she could have looked after all the animals.

"I'm trying to stop," I said, and sat up.

"Try to relax and have some fun this week," Sophie said. She pulled back the covers of her bed and climbed in. Making herself comfortable, she switched off the lamp by her bed. "I certainly plan to, and I'm going to make it my job to see that you do, too."

"I have been duly warned," I said, grinning down at her. She stuck out her tongue.

"Go on and get ready for bed," she said. "I'm ready to go to sleep."

Her eyelids drooped even as she spoke, and she snuggled into the bed. I knew she would be sound asleep in three minutes. I had always envied this ability to drop off to sleep so quickly. She slept very soundly, too, unlike me. I was a restless sleeper, and I usually woke up at least twice a night. Of course, having nocturnal animals sharing the bed with me didn't help.

Ten minutes later, with the lights out, I, too, was in bed. I lay in the darkness, willing myself to relax, but it wasn't working. My head was buzzing too much with the events of the day, and I couldn't stop myself from replaying some of them. Avery Trowbridge appeared to be a flash point for controversy and dissension, but it hadn't seemed to bother him all that much.

After half an hour of this, I had at last begun to feel drowsy. Enjoying the floating feeling of imminent sleep, I cleared my mind to let the sleep come.

When the voices began to speak to me, I knew I was dreaming. I could make out two different voices, though the pitch was distorted somehow. The voices had an odd, tinny quality, and I struggled to make out the words.

They talked for some time before the volume grew louder. One of the voices seemed to be quite angry. I could almost make out the words. I had the feeling I should be paying more attention to what they were saying, but the effort was too much for my relaxed state. The voices stopped talking, and there was another sound. After that, silence. I drifted off.

"Emma, wake up," a voice called to me. "Come on, Emma, time to get up for breakfast."

"Go away," I mumbled as I turned away from the sound of the voice.

"Emma, it's already seven thirty, and you have that bridge lesson at nine. Don't you want to get up and have some breakfast first?" I felt a hand on my shoulder, and startled by the touch, I came awake.

"Sophie," I said, lying on my back and blinking up at her. "Have you been talking to someone else?"

Sophie shook her head, laughing. "No, I haven't. I've just been trying to wake you up, sleepyhead. Now, come on and get out of bed. You'll be late if you don't get going."

I sat up, trying to clear my head. The last thing I remembered last night, I had heard two people talking. I was so sure they had been close to me, but in the light of day I realized how foolish that was. It was a dream, I decided as I threw back the covers and swung my feet to the floor.

Standing in the space between the two beds, I stretched a couple of times. I had slept pretty well, and I felt refreshed this morning. I turned back to the bed, grabbing the covers and pulling them up over the pillows. I hated to leave the bed messy, even though I knew someone would be in to make it later.

As I twitched the bedcovers into place, I stared at the wall across from me. There was a large air vent there. I gazed at it a few moments longer as an idea struck me. On the other side of this wall was the next suite.

Perhaps I really had heard a conversation last night. I could have heard voices coming through the air vent, because I figured there was a twin to this vent in the same place in the wall in the next suite.

I sniffed the air. I had caught a whiff of an unpleasant scent. What could it be? The smell reminded me of something.

"Emma."

I turned and saw Sophie standing in the doorway of our bathroom. "I'm done in here. Now, come on and get ready. I'm hungry, and I want my breakfast."

"Come here a minute," I called to Sophie. "Do you smell something funny?"

Sophie stepped closer until she stood near me. She sniffed audibly. "No, not really, but I just got through putting on perfume. Why? What do you smell?"

I shrugged. "Something odd, but I guess it's gone now. Maybe it was a mouse in the wall."

"Yuck," Sophie said, wrinkling her nose in disgust. "I don't want to think about that. Come on, and get ready. I want breakfast."

Laughing, I threw up my hands in a gesture of surrender. "Okay, you win. I'm going to hop into the shower right now, I promise. I'll be ready to go in fifteen minutes." I glanced back at the air vent. "But just to be safe, when I go downstairs, I think I'd better tell someone at the front desk there might be a dead mouse in the air vent."

Sophie grimaced again before pointing toward the bathroom. I took the hint.

I lived up to my promise, because fifteen minutes later, at ten minutes to eight, I followed Sophie out of our bedroom to the door of the suite.

"What about Marylou? Have you talked to her this morning?"

Sophie shook her head. "I peeked in on her a few minutes ago, and she was sound asleep. I'm betting she played bridge until after midnight, but she'll be up in time to play again this morning. I think the duplicate sessions start at nine thirty."

We were stepping into the hall when the phone rang in our bedroom. "Oh, just let it ring," Sophie said. "I doubt it's anything important."

"No, let me get it," I said, hurrying back into the suite. "It'll just take a minute."

Sighing, Sophie stepped back inside to wait.

I picked up the phone on about the fourth ring.

"Hello," I said.

"Emma, is that you?" It was Jackie, the cat sitter.

"Yes, Jackie, it's me," I said, and my stomach began to knot up. Something was wrong with one of the cats.

"It's not an emergency," Jackie said, responding to the note of concern in my voice.

"What is it?" Sophie had followed me to the door of our bedroom.

"Hang on a second, Jackie," I said. Covering the mouthpiece with one hand, I told Sophie, "You go on down to breakfast. It's Jackie. I'll talk to her and then I'll come down and join you."

"Is everything okay?"

"She said it's not an emergency," I replied. I motioned for her to go on. Shaking her head slightly, she turned and disappeared.

"Sorry, Jackie, I was just telling Sophie to go on to breakfast. Now, what's going on?"

"The cats are fine," Jackie said. "I didn't mean to alarm you by calling you so early."

"That's okay," I said, relieved. "If the cats are fine, though, is something else wrong?"

"It's my mother," Jackie said, sounding apologetic. "She lives in Dallas, and she's got to go into the hospital for some tests. My mother wants me to come and stay with her, and I can't say no."

"Well, of course," I said. "I understand completely. Your place is with your mother."

"Thank you," Jackie said. "I wanted to let you know about it, and I also wanted to let you know that I've arranged for a good friend of mine to take over for me." She paused, and when I didn't respond immediately, she went on, "I've known her for over twenty years, and she loves cats. I know she'll take really good care of Olaf and Hilda for you."

"Jackie," I said, "if you vouch for her, then I'm sure she'll be just fine. I appreciate your taking care of this. You go on to Dallas and look after your mother."

"Thanks, Emma," Jackie said, sounding greatly relieved. "Kathy has your numbers, and I'm going to take her over to your place to meet Olaf and Hilda. I'll go over everything with her there, and then I'll head for Dallas."

"Drive carefully," I said. I didn't envy Jackie the long and boring drive from Houston to Dallas.

After another round of assurances on both sides, we hung up. I had a few qualms about my cats being in the care of someone I had never met, but I did trust Jackie's judgment. So I fussed at myself for being a worrywart.

"Go get yourself some breakfast," I said aloud. "You'll feel better once you've had some coffee."

I left the bedroom, trying not to laugh at myself. I paused for a moment in the living room. Still no peep out of Marylou's room.

Stepping out into the hall, I pulled the door shut quietly behind me. As I moved down the hall toward the elevator, I glanced to my left at Avery Trowbridge's door. I remembered the voices I thought I had dreamed last night, and I wondered again whether what I heard had come from this suite.

I stopped in front of Trowbridge's door. There were six pieces of paper taped to his door, two across and three down. Examining them briefly, I saw that they were schedules of his lessons, and I saw my name, along with those of Bart and Bob, in the nine o'clock slot for this morning.

Then I realized the door was every so slightly ajar, and for some reason, that struck me as strange. After a moment's hesitation I stepped closer to the door and put my ear near the opening.

Not a sound to be heard from inside.

But I did catch a whiff of an unpleasant odor—the same one I had smelled in our bedroom just a short time ago.

I debated with myself over what I should do, and curiosity won. I had to investigate, because Avery Trowbridge could be ill in there and too weak to get to a phone. At least, that was how I justified it to myself.

I pushed the door open with my shoulder. Some instinct told me not to touch anything. The smell grew stronger, and I had a very bad feeling that I knew what it was. I tried to breathe as shallowly as I could. I remembered now where I had smelled it before. It was the smell of something dead.

The lights were on, and as I moved slowly forward, I could see that the floor plan of this suite was different from ours. In front of me was a living room, and to the right was a door into a bedroom. This appeared to be a one-bedroom suite, unlike ours.

I scanned slowly to my left, and my heart nearly stopped when I spotted someone sprawled in a chair in the corner of the room. The chair, a large leather wingback, partially obscured my view, but there was something unnatural about the position of the person in it.

Without even thinking, I took about three steps toward him, but then I halted. I clapped my hand over my nose and mouth, trying to filter out the stench that grew stronger the closer I came to the chair.

The person in the chair was Avery Trowbridge, and he was dead. The handle of a knife protruded from his chest.

Chapter 10

I couldn't move, nor could I tear my eyes away from the horrible sight of Avery Trowbridge's corpse. There were a few flies buzzing around him, and a fair amount of blood had dripped from the wound in his chest down his stomach and onto his legs. Some of it had spattered onto the carpet.

Trowbridge's head was turned away from me, and I couldn't see his face completely, but there was no doubt in my mind it was he. I shuddered. I needed to get out of here before I started throwing up.

As I took a step backward, I noted something odd. I halted.

Clutched in Trowbridge's hand, which rested on his right leg, was a playing card. Then for the first time I saw the table to the left of the chair where the corpse sat. Cards lay on the table as if a bridge game had been in progress.

My eyes skittered back to the card in Trowbridge's hand. The face of it was turned toward me, and I noted dimly that it was the queen of diamonds.

I was startled by hearing a voice behind me.

"Good grief, Avery, what is that awful smell?"

I turned, having recognized Paula Trowbridge's voice.

She stood blinking at me, clutching a large purse in her right hand.

"Emma, what are you doing here? Are you supposed to be having a lesson with Avery?" Her nose wrinkled in disgust. "What *is* that smell?"

I realized that I was blocking her view of her husband's corpse, and with that realization I went into action. I stepped forward quickly, trying to shield her from the dead body. I wanted to hustle her out of the room before she had time to see anything.

Grabbing her by the shoulders, I succeeded in turning her in the direction of the door before she realized what I was doing. I put my hands back in place on her shoulders and urged her forward. Her handbag banged against my legs.

"What are you doing?" She tried to stop and turn around, but I guess my adrenaline was pumping so hard that I was much stronger than she was. I muscled her out of the suite and into the hall.

She stumbled to a halt, and I let go of her. She whirled around, her face red and her chest heaving. "Just what the hell is going on here? And what was that god-awful smell? What have you and Avery been up to?" She brushed past me, and again she banged her purse into me. "I'm going back in there."

"No, you're not." I grabbed her arm and held on, pulling her toward me forcefully. I caught her in midstride, and she lost her balance slightly. She stumbled against me, and I wrapped my arms around her.

"Listen to me, Paula," I said in the tone I used to take with my misbehaving students. "You cannot go in there. You've got to come with me." Still holding on to her, I started marching her next door to my suite.

"There's something wrong with Avery, isn't there?"

Paula stopped resisting me for a moment, and I managed to move her a few feet closer to my door.

"Yes, there is," I said, "Right now there's nothing we can do for him. We need to call the police."

"Police?" Paula nearly shrieked the word. "What happened? Why do we need the police?"

"Just come with me, and I'll explain," I said, trying to use a calming tone. I didn't want any other residents of this floor to overhear us and come out to see what was going on.

Finally docile, Paula came with me to my door, and I fumbled in my pocket for the key. I glanced at her, and her face was pale.

"Don't faint on me," I said as I stuck the key into the lock.

"I won't," Paula said. She clutched her purse to her chest.

I gave her a slight push to get her into the room, and once she was inside, she made a beeline for the couch and almost threw herself on it, dropping her handbag on the floor. She started sobbing.

Marylou stepped into the room, pulling a dressing gown around her and tying the sash. "What on earth is the matter?" She glanced from me to Paula.

"Can you look after her?" I said, nodding my head toward Paula. "Something has happened next door. Avery Trowbridge is dead, and I need to let the hotel know."

Startled, Marylou stared at me for a few seconds, but then, without a word, she advanced on Paula.

I went to the desk near the window and picked up the phone. My hand was steady as I punched the zero. I felt cold all over, but, for the moment at least, completely in control of myself.

"Good morning," a female voice said into my ear. "How may I help you?"

Relieved that the voice didn't belong to Veronica Hinkelmeier, I quickly identified myself. "I've just discovered a dead body in the next suite. It's Avery Trowbridge, and he's been murdered."

For a moment there was no reply. When it came, the voice was obviously shaken. "Good Lord. This isn't some kind of prank, is it?"

"No, I assure you it is not," I said, once again using my teacher voice. "You need to call the police right away."

"Sheriff's department," the woman said, obviously still a bit dazed by my news. "We're outside the city limits."

"Well, whoever, then," I replied, beginning to lose patience. "Just do it. They need to get here as quickly as possible." I dropped the receiver into its cradle.

"Murder?" Marylou said. I turned around. Marylou was sitting on the couch, Paula's head resting on her left shoulder. The crying woman clung to her friend like she was a life preserver.

"I'm afraid so," I said.

"Oh, dear me," Marylou said. She patted Paula's back with one hand and stroked her hair with the other. "Shush, now, Paula, and try to get ahold of yourself."

"I forgot to tell them to send someone to guard the door," I said, annoyed with myself. I started to pick up the phone but stopped. Surely the woman to whom I had spoken had sense enough to realize that.

"I'm going back next door," I said. "Someone needs to watch that door until the sheriff's department gets here."

"Oh, dear," Marylou said again, looking very troubled.

"You keep an eye on her," I said. "I'll be okay."

I went back out in the hall and moved quickly to stand near the door of the dead man's suite. I glanced inside to be certain that no one was in there, and, satisfied, I turned my back to the door. I had left it open when I took Paula next door, and I figured I should just leave it open now. I shouldn't risk touching the door again, despite the smell.

"What's going on?"

I looked down the hall to see Leonard, the bellboy or whatever he was, approaching. He halted in front of me.

"Avery Trowbridge is dead," I said.

"Ohmigod," Leonard said. He made as if to step around me into the room, and I put up a hand. "What's that awful smell?"

"Don't go in there. You don't want to contaminate the crime scene."

"Crime scene?" Leonard's voice rose to a high note on the second word. "Ohmigod." He paled. "All she told me was that someone died. Maybe I should take a look."

"Trust me," I said, "you don't really want to see what's in there." He gave in without further protest and simply stood there staring at me.

Thus far I had managed to block what I had seen from my mind, but now it all came back, along with the smell. Maybe I should try to close the door after all. Turning, I put my full weight on my right leg and hooked the door with my left foot and pulled it toward me. Seeing what I was doing, Leonard put his arm on my right shoulder to steady me. I got the door as close to shut as I could, then let go.

"That's better," I said.

Leonard, his nose wrinkling in disgust, nodded. "That smell," he said.

"Try not to think about it," I told him. Advice that I wished I could follow myself. *Think about pleasant things,* I told myself. *Don't let your mind go there.* Time enough later to fall apart from the horror of what I had seen.

"I'll stand guard if you like," Leonard said. The color was coming back into his face. "I promise I won't go in there, and I won't let anyone else go in there either."

He seemed a trustworthy sort, and I decided to accept his offer. My stomach was not calming down. "Thanks," I said. "I'll be next door."

He ducked his head in acknowledgment.

I practically ran back to our suite. I had left the door open, and I hurried through it and through the living room to the bathroom. I was distinctly queasy, and I feared I might not make it in time.

I dropped to me knees by the toilet. I couldn't suppress any longer the horrible images of what I had seen. I threw up a couple of times, had a few dry heaves, and then it was over.

I sat by the toilet until I felt strong enough to stand. My hands were shaky as I turned the cold-water tap. I soaked a hand towel with water and held it against my face. The coolness felt wonderful. I stood that way for a minute or two, and then put the towel away.

Grabbing a cup, I filled it with water and swilled the water around in my mouth. I spit that out and repeated the procedure. I debated rinsing my mouth with some mouthwash, but I thought the smell might bother me.

I dried my face before I went back into the living

room. Paula, no longer sobbing, sat beside Marylou on the sofa, clutching her hand.

"Are you okay, Emma?" Marylou asked me.

I nodded. "Just a little queasy, but otherwise okay."

Marylou looked like she wanted to ask me questions, but she thought better of it.

"I'll tell you about it later," I said.

She nodded.

"What happened?" Paula spoke in a harsh, low voice.

"Someone killed your husband," I said, trying to be gentle.

"But who would want to kill him?" Paula asked, shaking her head. "Why would anyone do such a thing?"

I stared at her in disbelief. She had to be kidding. After all that I had witnessed since meeting her dead husband, I could think of several reasons why someone would kill him, including Paula herself. Now was perhaps not the time to remind her that she herself had threatened his life during that phone conversation Sophie and I overheard at Marylou's house.

There were sounds of commotion coming from the hallway. I went to the door, which I had left open in my dash for the bathroom. Peering into the hall, I saw several people in uniform at the neighboring door talking to Leonard.

I ducked back into the room and sat down in a chair near the sofa. "The sheriff's department is here," I said.

Paula stood up, finally letting go of Marylou's hand. "I should go and talk to them," she said. "Shouldn't I?" She looked down at Marylou.

"I think you should sit still and wait until they want to talk to you," Marylou said in a firm tone. "They're going to be too busy for a little while, and they'll get to you soon enough."

"She's right," I said. "Let's just sit tight until they come looking for us." I wasn't in any hurry to tell my story to anyone official, because I knew it would take a long time and I would be completely exhausted by the time it was over.

My stomach rumbled, and my head ached. I hadn't had any coffee yet, and the caffeine withdrawal was beginning to hit me. I didn't think I could face food for a while yet, but I sure could use some coffee.

"I'm going to make some coffee," I said. Our suite had a minibar, and I had noticed a regular-sized coffeemaker there. "Who else wants some?" I got up from my chair and went to the minibar and started rummaging around.

"I could use some," Marylou said, sighing. "It'll probably be forever before we can have any breakfast."

"Me, too, I guess," Paula said. "Maybe with a shot of brandy in it?"

"I'll see," I told her. First I concentrated on getting the coffee started, and once that was done, I opened the small cabinet in the minibar and located a little bottle of brandy. "Here we are." I set the bottle on top of bar.

I stood at the minibar, and Marylou and Paula sat on the sofa. We could hear sounds of activity from next door, but none of us spoke. The gurgling of the coffeemaker and our own breathing were the only sounds in the room.

Voices came to us from the hall, but I couldn't really make out what they were saying.

Voices.

Suddenly I remembered the voices I had heard last

night when I was trying to go to sleep. I had been in a pretty hazy state at the time, but I thought I recalled there was an argument going on. Then, abruptly, there had been silence before I drifted off completely.

My breath quickened as the realization hit me.

Without knowing it, I had been listening to a murder.

Chapter 11

I probably heard Avery Trowbridge being murdered.

For a moment I thought I was going to have to dash for the bathroom again. Instead I gripped the edge of the minibar tightly and willed my stomach to stop lurching about. I told myself I was being ridiculous. I'd had a strange dream, and more than likely it had nothing to do with Avery Trowbridge's death.

The problem was, I didn't believe myself. My so-called dream was too much of a coincidence.

"Emma, honey, what's wrong?" Marylou said. "You're white as a sheet right now."

"I'm okay," I said, though my voice came out as a croak. I cleared my throat. "Really, I'm okay. It's just a lot to take in right now." I attempted a smile. "Once I have some coffee, I'll feel a lot better."

"Of course," Marylou said, but she didn't look like she believed me. Then she glanced down at herself. "Oh my goodness, here I am still in my nightclothes. I'd better get dressed before the police come wanting to talk to us." She patted Paula's hand as she got up from the couch. "You just stay here with Emma."

Paula nodded. Marylou trudged off to her bedroom and shut the door behind her.

I eyed the coffeemaker and said, "Coffee's almost ready."

"Good," Paula replied. "I'm feeling cold."

"How do you take it?"

"Black is fine."

I poured us each a mug of coffee and handed Paula hers, having added some brandy. To my own I added some sugar and cream. Adding the sugar made me remember something.

"Paula, maybe you should have some sugar in your coffee."

She looked at me inquiringly.

"It's good for someone who might be suffering from shock," I explained. "It can't hurt, just in case."

Paula thrust her mug at me. "Sure, why not? I don't feel so good."

I added a generous amount of sugar, stirred it in, then gave Paula back her coffee. She sipped at it. "Oh, that's good. I'm feeling warmer already."

I didn't reply. I watched her as I sipped at my own coffee. Caffeine on an upset stomach probably wasn't the best idea, but at least my headache ebbed away as I drank.

I was surprised at Paula. Frankly, I had been expecting all kinds of histrionics over the murder of her husband. But perhaps she was relieved he was out of the way, and was afraid of giving that away if she said anything. She was hard to figure out.

"What's going on next door? Is that why you didn't come down to breakfast?" Sophie had walked into the room without my hearing her—I had been so intent on Paula.

Sophie approached the bar and thrust a Styrofoam container at me. "I brought you some breakfast," she said. She settled on a stool at the breakfast bar. "Now, tell me what's going on."

"Thank you," I said as I accepted the food. I opened the container and glanced inside. Biscuits and sausage, plus a couple of small cinnamon buns. Good. Those I could deal with. If Sophie had brought me scrambled eggs—I shuddered at the thought. I clamped the top down and answered Sophie's question.

"Avery Trowbridge has been murdered," I said, keeping my voice low. "I found the body."

"Ohmigod," Sophie said, paling. "I figured it had to be something pretty serious. They didn't want to let me pass by them, and when I asked them why, they wouldn't answer. I finally talked them into it, saying I needed to look after a sick friend. Plus I showed them my room key. I guess I finally wore them down, although it probably only took about three minutes."

A knock sounded at the door before I could reply to her. Sophie slid off the stool and went to the door. "Who is it?" she called.

"Sheriff's department," was the answer.

Sophie opened the door and stepped back to let someone enter.

Actually, it was two someones—a tall, broad-shouldered, heavyset man and a woman whose height matched his. He looked to be in his fifties, while the woman was about twenty years younger. Both were in uniform, and I could hear the leather they wore creaking as they walked into the room.

"I'm Deputy Ainsworth, and this is Deputy Jordan," the man announced. "I'm in charge of the investigation." He paused a moment to look from Sophie to Paula and finally to me. "I understand one of you ladies found the body."

"Yes, that was me," I said, coming around the mini-bar and standing close to where Sophie stood. "I'm Emma Diamond. This is my friend Sophie Parker. And the lady on the couch is Paula Trowbridge, Mrs. Avery Trowbridge."

Deputy Ainsworth stared at Paula for a moment. "That's your husband in there." It wasn't really a question.

Paula nodded. She tried to speak but couldn't. She took a sip of her coffee and tried again. "Yes, Deputy, Avery was my husband."

"Sorry for your loss, ma'am." The deputy's voice was gruff, almost raspy. He sounded like a heavy smoker.

Ainsworth focused on me again. "Ms. Diamond," he began.

"Mrs. Diamond," I corrected him. "I'm a widow." He had an odd look on his face as he regarded me.

The deputy nodded. "Mrs. Diamond, I need to get a statement from you. Would you mind stepping out in the hall with me?"

"Not at all, Deputy. Do you mind if I bring my coffee with me?"

"Go right ahead, ma'am." He moved to the door and held it open. "Jordan will stay here with the other ladies. I'd appreciate it if y'all didn't talk about the incident until I've had a chance to question you separately."

Sophie and Paula nodded.

I stepped into the hallway, and Deputy Ainsworth closed the door behind us. He guided me to the large window at the end of the hall. He stood with his back to the window; I faced it. The sun coming through the glass was warm, and it felt good. Despite the coffee, I was still a little cold. Perhaps I was suffering a bit from shock.

Behind me I could hear the low hum of conversation coming from Avery Trowbridge's room, along with other noises. I was glad I had my back to it all. I really didn't want to see anything else that was taking place in that room. I shuddered and took another sip of coffee.

Ainsworth was watching me with that same enigmatic expression. "Mrs. Diamond, I'd like you to tell me what happened this morning. How you came to find the body. Take your time."

Clasping my mug with both hands, I thought for a moment before speaking. "I was on my way down to breakfast. It was a few minutes before eight, I think. Anyway, my friend Sophie Parker had gone down ahead of me, and I was going to join her." I paused for a breath. "I was walking down the hall, and when I neared Mr. Trowbridge's room, I suppose I noticed the pieces of paper taped to his door."

When I didn't go on immediately, Ainsworth prompted me. "They look like a schedule of some kind."

I nodded. "Yes, Mr. Trowbridge is, er, was a famous bridge player and teacher. He was giving lessons, beginning this morning. I had signed up for the first slot at nine. I guess I was curious, so I stopped to peruse the schedule, and I could see that it was pretty full." I stopped for a deep breath and another sip of coffee.

"That was when I noticed the door ever so slightly ajar. Plus there was an odd smell coming from the room." For a moment, I could smell it again, but I stuck the mug under my nose and inhaled the aroma of coffee instead.

Ainsworth regarded me sympathetically. "What did you do next?"

"I pushed the door open," I said. "With my shoulder." I shrugged. "I sensed something was wrong, and I didn't want to touch anything."

The deputy frowned. I waited for him to comment, but he simply gestured for me to continue.

"I walked into the room, and of course the smell was a lot a stronger there. I started looking around, and then I saw that someone was slumped in the chair in the corner. I took a few steps toward the chair, and I could see flies buzzing around. And the smell." I closed my eyes, and it all came back to me.

I must have looked like I was going to faint, because Ainsworth put a steadying hand on my arm.

"I'm okay," I said, and opened my eyes. The deputy dropped his arm.

"Tell me what you saw."

I stared past Ainsworth, focusing on the trees outside. "Avery Trowbridge was in the chair, and there was a knife protruding from his chest. There was also a fair amount of blood." I paused. "I guess that means he didn't die for a while. That's right, isn't it? The heart had to be beating, pumping blood, because once the heart stopped, so would the flow of blood."

Ainsworth's expression would have been funny under other circumstances.

"I read a lot of mystery novels," I explained, a bit on the defensive. "You can pick up a lot of interesting information that way."

The deputy nodded. "So I've heard." He shifted his weight from one foot to the other. "What else did you see?"

"Cards were laid out on the table, as if there was a bridge game in progress," I said. "And Trowbridge had one card in his hand."

"Did you see what it was?"

"The queen of diamonds," I said.

Ainsworth nodded. He had that odd look on his face again. "I'm going to ask you not to tell anyone else what you saw. Of course, people will know you found the body, but I'm asking you not to give details of what you saw to anyone."

"I understand," I said. "I won't say anything." I watched him watching me. The coincidence of my name and the card clutched in the dead man's hand had disconcerted him somehow. And I knew why.

I had learned from my extensive reading of mystery fiction that the police often suspected the person who found the body. Given that, along with my last name and the card in the corpse's hand, it was no wonder that Deputy Ainsworth was looking at me with suspicion.

That in turn made me start to wonder whether the card had any significance. Was it simply the card Trowbridge was holding when he was stabbed, and in his death throes he held on to it?

Or did he pick up the card after he had been stabbed, intending to leave some kind of clue to the identity of his killer? I knew already, by the amount of blood I had seen, that he hadn't died immediately. He could have had time to pick up a card from the table before he died.

It seemed outlandish, and yet I thought it was at least possible.

"What did you do next?" Ainsworth's voice broke into my train of thought.

"I was about to leave the room to call the authorities," I said. "But then Mrs. Trowbridge—Paula, that is—came into the room and spoke from behind me. I didn't want her to see her husband lying there murdered, so I got her out of the room as quickly as I could."

"So you don't think she saw anything?"

"I'm not completely certain, but I was standing in the way of her view of the body. She resisted me a little, because I'm sure she thought I was acting like a lunatic. But I got her out of the room into the hall, and then into my suite next door." I drained the last of my coffee from the mug and wished I could refill it.

"I notified the hotel staff and told them they needed to call the authorities," I said. "Then I realized that someone should probably keep an eye on the room. I had left the door wide open when I got Paula out of there, and I didn't think it would be good for someone else to come along and wander inside."

Ainsworth was doing his best to keep his face blank, but once again I thought I could read his mind. If I were the killer, I would want time to get back in the room before the authorities arrived and do whatever it was I needed to do.

"I didn't go back in the room," I said as calmly as I could, though I was getting a bit rattled, I must confess. "I was there only for a minute or two before Leonard, one of the hotel staff, arrived. I pulled the door shut as far as I could with my foot, and Leonard kept watch until you arrived. He promised he wouldn't go in the room."

"Thank you, Mrs. Diamond," Ainsworth said. "You've been pretty clear in what you've told me. I'll probably have more questions for you later."

I hesitated for a moment. Should I tell him about the voices I heard last night? Or would he simply think I was trying to give myself some sort of alibi by claiming to have heard someone else kill Avery Trowbridge?

Chapter 12

"Is there something else you'd like to tell me?" Ainsworth's eyes narrowed as he regarded me.

I sighed inwardly. Now I had little choice. "I heard something last night that might be relevant."

"What was it?"

"It was while I was trying to go to sleep last night," I said. "I was lying in bed, in kind of a hazy state. Not totally awake, and not quite asleep, either."

Ainsworth nodded, waiting for me to continue.

"Well, while I was drifting off, I heard voices. I couldn't tell what they were saying, but they talked for a while. At some point the voices got louder, but I still couldn't really make out what they were saying. And then there was silence."

"If these voices were real, and not just a part of some dream you were having," Ainsworth said after a brief silence, "where were they coming from?"

"From Avery Trowbridge's room, I'm pretty sure," I answered. "My bed is next to the common wall between the two suites. There's a large air vent in that wall, right by my bed, and there's an air vent in the same place on the other side of the wall. I noticed it this morning. The voices must have come through there, but the sound was muffled, distorted even."

Ainsworth considered that for a moment. "We'll have to check that out. But you're sure you didn't hear anything that the voices were saying?"

"No, none of it was distinct enough. There was just an abrupt silence when the voices stopped, and then I must have really gone to sleep." I didn't say that I now thought I probably overheard the murder taking place, even though I had no idea what was going on at the time.

"And then, this morning, I thought I smelled something unpleasant through the vent." I shuddered. "Now I know what it was."

The deputy stared at me without saying anything for what seemed an eternity. For a few moments there, I was convinced I was about to be hauled off to the sheriff's department to be charged with murder. Alternatively, to the closest mental health facility.

"How well did you know the victim?"

Ainsworth's question startled me a bit because it was not the response I was expecting. He actually should have asked me that earlier, and I wondered why he hadn't.

"I met him for the first time yesterday," I said. "I'd never even heard of him until a few days ago."

"How did you hear about him?"

"Through his wife, Paula Trowbridge." I gestured toward my suite. "And I met her through a mutual friend, Marylou Lockridge, whom you met. Paula was visiting Marylou in Houston, and I'm Marylou's next-door neighbor. Sophie Parker, my best friend, lives on the other side of me. I've known Sophie since she was a little girl. Sophie is here, too, sharing the bedroom with me. Marylou is in the other bedroom in the suite."

I forced myself to stop babbling, but Ainsworth's intent gaze had disconcerted me. I imagined it was probably a technique he used to wring confessions out of criminals. It certainly had its effect on me, making me jabber like an idiot.

"So you haven't known Mrs. Trowbridge very long either," Ainsworth stated.

"No, only a few days." I clamped my mouth shut after those few words. I wasn't going to let my lips loose again.

"What did you think of the victim?" Ainsworth continued to bore into me with his eyes. "You say you only met him yesterday, but you must have formed some kind of opinion of him."

I had to be careful what I said. At some point I would probably have to tell him the various things I had witnessed, but I didn't think now was the proper time.

"He seemed like a man who stirred up strong feelings in people," I said. "Particularly in women."

The ghost of a smile played across the deputy's lips.

"Frankly," I continued, "I found him more than a bit obnoxious."

"But you were signed up to have a lesson with him this morning."

I nodded. "Yes, I had signed up for one. Just because I found him annoying didn't mean I couldn't learn something about bridge from him. He was a celebrity in the bridge world, and I don't imagine he achieved that without a very high level of skill at playing bridge." I shrugged. "Besides, I was supposed to share the lesson with two other people, both men. I wouldn't have been alone with him." I didn't want to tell this police officer that booking the lesson was mostly curiosity on my part.

Ainsworth stood in silence for a moment, staring past me at something or someone. I resisted the urge to turn and look.

"I think that's all for now," he finally said to me. He stared at me a moment. "Unless there's something else you've forgotten to tell me."

I shook my head. "No, that's it."

"Right." He took my elbow and steered me toward the door of my suite. "I want to talk to Mrs. Trowbridge now. Would you mind if I interviewed her in your suite? Is there another room you and the other lady could go to while I talk to her?"

I pushed open the door and walked into the living room. Marylou and Paula were sitting in silence on the sofa, while Ainsworth's junior deputy stood to attention near the window. Sophie sat at the breakfast bar. "We can go into Marylou's bedroom," I said in a low voice.

"Thank you," Ainsworth said. He stepped past me. "Mrs. Trowbridge."

Paula looked up at him. "Yes?"

"I'd like to talk to you right now. I'm very sorry for your loss, and I know this is distressing for you, but it would really help me if I could ask you some questions."

"Whatever," Paula said in an offhand manner. Ainsworth might have just asked her whether she liked dogs. I stared at her for a moment, trying to read her. She really was the most peculiar woman.

"Marylou, Sophie, let's go into Marylou's room," I said, motioning for Marylou and Sophie to come with me. "The deputy needs to talk to Paula alone."

Sophie hopped off her stool and walked into Marylou's bedroom. Marylou hesitated, but she followed Sophie. I shut the door behind us, then leaned against it. Marylou walked over to her bed and sagged down onto it. Sophie perched on the other side of the bed.

"How is she taking it?" I asked. I heard the murmur of voices in the living room, but I couldn't make out what they were saying. There was no point in lingering by the door any longer, so I made myself comfortable in the overstuffed armchair near Marylou's bed.

"I think she's still in shock," Marylou said uncertainly. "Of course, we couldn't really talk with that deputy watching over us, but I don't think Paula would have said much even if she could."

"You're right," Sophie said. "I kept watching her face, and I would swear that most of the time nobody was home. I've never seen such a blank expression on anybody's face before. It's like she just shut down." She grimaced.

"Maybe that's the way she copes with things," I commented. "Some people turn completely inward at times like this."

"I guess you're right," Sophie said, "but she still gives me the willies."

"What do you think, Marylou?" I asked.

She shrugged. "I guess you're right, Emma. Paula is prone to dramatizing herself, but she's always been good at shutting out anything that she didn't want to deal with. She's good at denial."

"I don't think she can deny this," Sophie said. "Someone murdered her husband."

"Do you think she did it?" I asked, looking at Sophie and Marylou in turn.

Sophie spoke first. "She could have, I guess, but why would she? I mean, I know she wanted a divorce from the guy, but it's not like divorces aren't easy to get. This isn't Victorian England, for Pete's sake."

"Unless he was worth a lot of money that she could inherit," I said, thinking about it. "If she divorced him, she couldn't get her hands on all of it."

Sophie and I waited for Marylou to say something. When she realized that both of us were staring at her, she spoke. "I just don't know what to think. You think you know someone, and something like this happens. I don't think Paula would kill anyone, or *could* kill anyone. But I just don't know. I don't think she would care about the money all that much. I think she just wanted to be free of him." She frowned. "And like Sophie says, she could have divorced him. She *wanted* to divorce him, but he was resisting, for some reason."

"There are certainly other people who might have had reasons to want him dead," I said.

"No kidding," Sophie said. "I can think of four right off the bat, and there are probably others that we know nothing about."

"Who's on your list?" I asked.

Sophie cocked her head, considering her response. "First, there's his ex-wife. She's a pretty cool customer, and I think she hated him. Then there's his son, who didn't seem to care much for him either. He might have stood to gain the most, at least where money's concerned. Or maybe Avery threatened to cut him off completely."

"From what we overheard," I said, "it sounded like Avery wasn't giving his son the financial support he needed."

Sophie nodded. "And his son could have been really angry about that. Get rid of Dad and then get his hands on Dad's money."

"That's possible," Marylou said.

"Who else?" I asked Sophie. "You said four." I was curious to know whether her four matched mine. They probably did.

"There's dear sweet Veronica, of course. There was obviously something going on between her and Avery, and 'hell hath no fury' and all that. She looked mad enough to kill last night, that's for sure." Sophie rolled her eyes. "I would like it to be her, just because she's such a bitch."

I had to laugh at that, and Marylou reluctantly joined in.

"Finally," Sophie said, "there's his manager. Avery had fired him, or at least, that's what we overheard him say."

"Yes, we did hear that," I said, "and Avery claimed his agent had caused him some serious financial problems. Maybe the agent had been embezzling from him, and Avery was threatening to go to the police," I said.

"That would be another good answer," Marylou said. Then she sighed heavily. "But I'm afraid you're forgetting someone. There's a fifth person who could be said to have a motive for killing Avery."

"Basil Dumont," Sophie and I said in unison after a moment's pause.

Marylou nodded. "There was no love lost between Basil and Avery. We all saw that—very publicly—last night. Basil has always been pretty mild mannered, but maybe he finally snapped. Avery could have pushed him too far for once."

"Good point," I said. "So there are five people besides Paula with possible strong motives for getting rid of Avery Trowbridge."

Sophie and Marylou nodded.

"The police have their work cut out for them," I said. "Plus I think I may be on the list of suspects myself."

"Why?" Sophie asked.

Quickly I explained about the card in Avery Trowbridge's hand. I had told Ainsworth I wouldn't tell anyone, but that didn't include my two best friends.

"So you think he could have been trying to leave a clue to the killer's identity?" Marylou frowned. "What could the queen of diamonds mean? We know *you* didn't kill him, Emma."

"Maybe the killer put the card in his hand to confuse everyone," Sophie suggested.

"I don't know," I said, "but I hope they get it sorted out soon."

Sophie and Marylou exchanged looks, then faced me.

"What?" I asked with a voice full of suspicion.

"Don't look at us like that," Sophie said. "You know you want to figure this out just as much as we do."

"Is that so?" I said, trying to sound haughty and slightly offended.

Sophie snorted. "Come off it, Emma. I know you too well."

"Besides," Marylou said, very earnestly, "I don't want Paula to be accused of something she didn't do. I can't help feeling sorry for her, and she's going to need my—our—support."

"Okay," I said. "I agree. We should keep our eyes and ears open. We might spot something that the sheriff's department could miss, but we have to be careful, or Ainsworth really will think I have something to hide."

"Of course," Sophie and Marylou said in unison.

"I'm not sure Deputy Ainsworth will be too happy if he finds out we're going to be helping him." I rolled my eyes, and Sophie laughed.

Before either Sophie or Marylou could respond to that, we were all startled by loud screams coming from the other room.

Chapter 13

"What on earth?" Marylou said, rising from the bed. "That sounded like Paula."

I made it to the door first, and I flung it open as another scream erupted from somewhere. Sophie and Marylou crowded behind me into the doorway so that I was forced to take a step into the room. Then all three of us stopped, aghast, as we took in the scene before us.

Ainsworth had his hands full with a struggling Veronica Hinkelmeier, who was trying, without success, to free herself from the deputy. The other deputy, whose name I blanked on for the moment, was similarly occupied with Paula.

"Be still!"

Ainsworth's deep voice rumbled through the room, and both Paula and Veronica ceased struggling for a moment.

"She started it," Veronica said. "Just look at my face. It's probably bleeding." Her chest heaved with exertion as she made another attempt to loosen herself from the deputy's iron grip. "I'm going to sue you for assault."

"You can't sue me if you're locked up for murdering my husband." Paula was yelling, but she stood still.

Veronica's face was turned away from us, but from what she had said, Paula must have struck her. Marylou, Sophie, and I continued to watch. I didn't think the deputies had seen us yet; they were so focused on holding on to the two combatants.

"Now, just calm down," Ainsworth said. He experimented with easing up his grip on Veronica, but she immediately started to pull away from him. "If I have to, I'll handcuff you. Do you understand me?"

Veronica nodded. I could tell by the set of her shoulders she was still furious, but evidently she had begun to cool down a bit. Ainsworth let go of her, and she stood still. He stepped away from her, only a pace or two, and she remained where she was.

"The same goes for you, Mrs. Trowbridge," he said. "Will you sit back down on the couch?"

Paula nodded. She was calm again, and her face had taken on that blank look we had seen earlier. The deputy let go of her, and she sank down on the couch.

"Just look at my face," Veronica said. She had been examining herself in the mirror over the minibar. "Look at this."

She had turned where we could see her, and I winced. I heard Sophie and Marylou both mutter something. There were four streaks of red on her cheek. Paula must have raked Veronica's face with her fingernails.

Behind me, I felt Marylou move away. I knew her well enough to understand that she was getting ready to administer some first aid to Veronica. I was surprised the deputy hadn't done something about that, but evidently he had other things on his mind.

"Mrs. Trowbridge," Ainsworth said in a calm, reasonable tone. "Would you like to explain to me why you attacked this woman?"

"Veronica Hinkelmeier." Veronica introduced herself. "I'm the customer-service manager for the hotel."

Ainsworth nodded. When Paula didn't speak, he said, "Why did you attack Ms. Hinkelmeier?"

For a moment, I thought Paula was catatonic and incapable of responding. Then she turned her face to look up at the deputy. For a moment, she appeared to be a tragically bereaved widow. "Because she killed my husband."

Veronica hissed, and Ainsworth hastily put himself between the two women.

"She's out of her mind," Veronica said. "Why would I kill the man?"

I didn't think she sounded at all convincing. It didn't even sound like she believed what she was saying. Paula just looked at her with contempt.

"You were sleeping with him, and he dumped you," Paula said. She might have been talking about the weather; she was so calm now. "You thought he would marry you once he and I got a divorce, but I've heard about how he treated you last night. He humiliated you, and you killed him."

"What happened last night?" Ainsworth said.

"Just what I said," Paula replied. "She made advances, in public, to my husband, and he rejected her right in front of everyone." Her mouth twisted in a malicious grin.

"Did you witness this?" Ainsworth asked her.

Paula shook her head. "No, but I sure heard about it."

"Who told you?"

Paula laughed. "Avery's first wife, Lorraine. She

saw the whole thing. We had a good laugh about it. Neither one of us could believe how ridiculously this woman was behaving."

Marylou pushed past me, and I saw she was carrying a box of antiseptic hand towels and a tube of some kind of ointment. While Paula was speaking, Veronica stood stock-still, her face composed in a rigid mask. When Marylou approached her, she pushed her away.

"Do I have to stand here and listen to this crazy woman go on like this?"

Ainsworth turned to Veronica. "Is that what happened last night, Ms. Hinkelmeier?"

"Avery and I had a public argument, that's true," Veronica said, the color rising in her face. "But I wasn't sleeping with him, I don't care what she says. I don't sleep with married men."

Paula snorted with laughter. "You don't sleep with anybody besides married men, from what I hear."

With a cry of rage, Veronica launched herself at Paula. Ainsworth was taken off guard, and Veronica almost knocked him off his feet. The other deputy, Jordan—I think that was her name—managed to get between the two women in time. Ainsworth recovered his balance, and he grabbed hold of Veronica before she could get to Paula.

"All right," he said, visibly angry. "That's enough." He nodded at his deputy, who pulled her handcuffs from her belt. Before Veronica realized just what was happening, she had her hands cuffed behind her back.

"What are you doing?" she said.

"I could charge you with assaulting an officer of the law," Ainsworth said, "and if you don't cool down, I'll do it." His fierce demeanor made an impression—finally—on Veronica, and reality began to sink in.

"Jordan, take Mrs. Trowbridge to her room," he said, then stopped. "I guess you can't do that."

"I wasn't staying in the same room as my husband," Paula informed him. "I have my own room." She gave him the number.

"Okay, then," Ainsworth continued. "Deputy Jordan will take you to your room, and you will stay there. Don't talk to anyone. I'll come and finish questioning you there."

Paula nodded. She stood, and Jordan took her arm and led her to the door.

Ainsworth turned back to Veronica. "Now, Ms. Hinkelmeier, you and I are going downstairs to have a little talk, and we'll see about some first aid for your face. If I take the cuffs off, are you going to behave?"

Veronica nodded. Tears rolled down her face, and for a moment, I felt sorry for her. I did have to wonder, though, if Paula wasn't right—that Veronica was the murderer.

"Ladies, if you'll excuse us," Ainsworth said, nodding in our direction.

"Of course," I muttered. He had probably known all along that we were standing there, and I felt like a child caught with her hand in some forbidden dish.

"Excuse me, Deputy," Sophie said as she followed Ainsworth and Veronica to the door. "Do we have to stay here? Can we go downstairs and play bridge, for example?"

Ainsworth paused in the doorway. He seemed to be considering the question. "I don't see why not. But I have to ask you not to talk about anything you've seen or heard. Is that clear?"

We each assured him that it was.

"Okay, then," he said. "I'll have more questions for

you later, but I'll know where to find you." He nodded at us before stepping into the hall.

Sophie shut the door behind him and Veronica before joining Marylou and me in the seating area. Marylou and I sank down on the couch, and Sophie chose a chair. We stared at one another for a moment. Then Marylou looked down at the first aid items in her hands. Shaking her head, she set them on the end table near her.

"That was certainly quite a little show," Sophie said.

"Paula was really aggressive, I thought," I said.

"She certainly was," Marylou replied. "It's a bit out of character for her. I've never known her to actually attack somebody like that, but under the circumstances . . ." Her voice trailed off.

"I suppose so," I said. "Although if she's capable of that kind of anger, then she could have killed Avery."

"No," Marylou said. "No, I can't see Paula as a murderer. I just can't." She shook her head.

I didn't want to upset her any further, so I decided not to pursue that line of thinking for the moment.

"It's all ghastly," Sophie said, with a knowing glance at me, "but I still can't help being fascinated by it. I mean, who did it, and all that."

"We're all too curious for our own good."

Marylou laughed. "Maybe so." Then she sobered. "But I am worried about Paula."

"The best thing we can do for her is to keep eyes and ears open like we said before."

Marylou nodded.

"Okay, girls," Sophie said, "I don't know about you, but I don't want to sit here in this suite any longer. Let's go play some bridge, how about it?" She stood up, hands on her hips, waiting for a response.

Marylou and I didn't demur—we were both ready for a change of scene.

In the hallway, we stared curiously at the activity going on next door as we passed by. There were various crime scene personnel at work, so we didn't linger. I tried not to think about what I had seen in that room. Playing bridge would be a good distraction, at least for now. I just hoped I wouldn't have nightmares about the crime scene tonight.

Once downstairs we made our way to the ballroom. I glanced at my watch, amazed to see that it was only about nine fifteen. Play was supposed to commence at nine thirty, so we weren't even late, despite what had happened.

"I'll see you later," Marylou said. She headed for the duplicate-bridge area.

Sophie and I surveyed the scene on the nonduplicate side. Most of the tables were already occupied by foursomes, but I spotted one empty table. "Shall we sit there?" I pointed. "And hope that two more people turn up?"

"Might as well," Sophie said.

We had barely seated ourselves when we saw two men approaching us.

"Good morning, ladies," Bob said. "Mind if we join you and play a little bridge?" He smiled.

"Please do," I said.

His companion, Bart, said, "If it's okay with you, ladies, Bob and I don't usually play as partners." The two men glanced at each other and grinned. "We find that it's easier to keep the peace that way."

Amused, I shook my head. "Not a problem." I had sat down across from Sophie at the table, but I moved to the chair to her right.

Bob sat down across from me, and Bart took the chair opposite Sophie. Two decks of cards, a scorepad, and pencil were on the table between the two men.

Bob picked up a deck and started shuffling. Sophie handed the other deck to Bart to shuffle.

Once he finished shuffling his deck, Bob set the cards down to his right. Bart did the same thing with his deck. Sophie slid them toward me, and I cut. Sophie then dealt out the cards.

"Do you play any particular conventions?" Bob asked. "Bart and I play the usual ones, but we don't go in for a lot of the really complicated ones people play when they play duplicate."

"I'm still pretty much a novice," I said as I organized my hand. "We play Stayman, and Blackwood, of course, and we usually play short club openers."

"Same here," Bart said. "What about transfers?"

"I've read about them," I said, "but we haven't really played with them." I nodded at Sophie. "Sophie might have. She's played more than I have."

"Yes," Sophie said. "They can be quite useful."

Bart beamed at us. "Shall I refresh your memory?"

Suppressing a smile, I said, "Please do." Once a teacher, always a teacher. I was like that myself.

"Okay, then," Bart said. "You use transfers if one partner opens one no-trump. If you respond without using transfers, you can end up with the stronger hand as the dummy, and that gives your opponents an edge. So the point of transfers is to allow you to play from the stronger hand, with the weaker hand as dummy."

Sophie and I nodded obediently to show that we understood.

"I open one no-trump," Bart continued, "and if Sophie has up to seven high card points and a five-card major, she would bid two of the suit below her major. If she has a good heart suit, she would say two diamonds. And if she has a good spade suit, she would say two hearts."

Sophie and I nodded again.

"If I like the suit Sophie is bidding, I respond with a two bid in the appropriate suit," Bart said. "If Sophie doesn't have many points, she passes on her next bid. If she has a stronger hand, enough for us perhaps to make game, she can bid two no-trump if her suit is a five-card suit. If it's six cards or longer, she would bid three in the suit. Then I could decide whether to play three no-trump or four hearts of four spades."

"Sounds easy enough," I said. "But let me clarify one thing. If I respond to your one no-trump bid with two clubs, that means Stayman. If I respond with two diamonds or two hearts, it's a transfer."

"Exactly," Bob said.

"Those are the basics of the transfer," Bart said. "We can go into the more complex issues if we need to. Does that sound okay?"

"That's fine," Sophie said. She examined her hand, then giggled. "One no-trump."

Bob grinned before responding, "No bid."

Bart surveyed his hand. "Two hearts."

I passed.

Sophie bid two spades, Bob passed again, and Bart said, "Three no-trump."

"No bid," I said.

"Four spades," Sophie declared.

After three passes, Sophie noted the bid on the scorepad.

As Bob was deciding on the first lead, he said, "Have y'all noticed there's something strange going on in the hotel this morning? We've seen some people in cop uniforms coming and going."

Sophie and I exchanged glances.

"Yes," I said. "We've noticed, too."

"I suppose we'll find out eventually," Bart said.

"We asked at the front desk, but the girl there—I think her name is Monica—just looked scared and said she couldn't talk about it. It's all very mysterious."

"Yes, it is," Sophie agreed. She and I exchanged covert glances. I knew we both would have liked to tell Bob and Bart what was going on, but we had told Deputy Ainsworth we wouldn't talk about the murder.

Bob played the queen of hearts, and Bart put down the dummy hand.

"It's too bad about our private lesson," Bart said. "Bob and I were really looking forward to it. I'm sure you were, too, Emma. Avery Trowbridge is such a well-known teacher."

"Maybe he'll reschedule," Bob said.

Sophie and I were careful not to look at each other this time. I noticed something odd about the men's remarks. They didn't know Avery Trowbridge was dead, but who had let them know the lesson was canceled? Perhaps someone from the sheriff's department had called them. I had to know for sure, though.

"How did you find out the lesson was canceled?" I said, trying to keep my tone nonchalant.

"A woman called us this morning," Bart said. He frowned. "At least I think it was a woman. It was early, and the voice was a bit odd, now that I think about it. Didn't you get a call, too?" He played the king of hearts, and Sophie played the ace on it. I played the two.

"What time did she call you?" I asked as Sophie gathered the cards and placed them in front of her. She appeared absorbed in her cards, but I knew she was waiting for the answer to my question as impatiently as I was.

"It was actually pretty early," Bob replied. "A bit too early, if you ask me." He shook his head. "It's a good thing Bart and I are so used to getting up at the crack of dawn—otherwise we would have been pretty annoyed."

"How early is pretty early?"

Bart frowned. "It was about seven thirty, wasn't it?"

Chapter 14

"Seven thirty-three, actually," Bob said with a smile.

Bart shook his head. "He's obsessed with time. He always knows exactly when something happens."

I stole a look at Sophie, and she was looking at me. The significance of what the two men had told us was startling. Surely it was the murderer who had called them? Or, at the very least, someone in cahoots with the killer?

Sophie focused on selecting a card to lead. When she played it, I gave it a cursory look as I decided what to pull from my own hand. I ought to be concentrating on the game we were playing, but I was still trying to sort out the implications of that phone call.

Then another thought struck me. No one had called *me* to cancel the lesson.

At least, I didn't think anyone had. I'd have to check the phones in our suite to see if someone had left a message. I was willing to bet, though, no one had called.

The question was, *why?* Did the killer not know I was scheduled for a lesson along with Bart and Bob? That didn't make any sense, though. If the killer knew they were scheduled, he or she would also have known I was scheduled. My name and room number were on the list, along with those of Bob and Bart.

Suddenly I went completely cold.

The killer wanted me to find the body.

That was the only explanation I could come up with—unless whoever killed Avery had simply made a mistake. I wasn't sure I believed that, though. If someone had planned this murder, had part of that plan included me finding the body?

Maybe the killer simply wanted Marylou, Sophie, or me—or maybe the three of us together—to find the body. Or was I putting too much significance into this?

"Emma, it's your turn again," Sophie said. "We're waiting."

"Um, sorry," I said, tuning back in to the game. I looked at the board. "What led?"

"I led the king of spades," Sophie answered. Another spade and a club lay on the table with her king.

"Sorry." I pulled my one remaining spade, the four, and dropped it on the table.

Sophie collected the trick and put it in front of her, along with the two others she had taken. She examined her hand, then the board.

"I'm up," she said, laying her hand on the board.

Bob, Bart, and I examined the cards, and we all agreed with her.

"Making seven," Sophie said, grinning.

"But only bidding four," Bart reminded her.

"Too bad, so sad," Bob said in a singsong voice. "You stopped the auction too soon." He wrinkled his nose at Bart.

Bob and I had both had very weak hands, and the one finesse Sophie had needed worked. Even the fact that I hadn't been paying much attention to the game hadn't really mattered.

Bob set the cards in front of Sophie, and she cut

them. As he picked them up to deal, he said, "It's our turn this time, Emma. Let's get a slam hand, too."

"And bid it," Bart reminded him with a grin.

When Bob had finished, I picked up my cards and assembled the hand. This time I had eleven high card points, and if my partner could open, we ought to have game somewhere, or close to it.

Bob looked at his cards and, with a sigh, passed.

Bart opened a heart.

I passed, and Sophie responded with two hearts. Bob passed again, and so did Bart.

"Two hearts," Sophie said, recording the bid on the scorepad.

I tried to pay more attention this time, but I couldn't keep my mind away from the murder. What Bob and Bart had told us was important, and Deputy Ainsworth ought to hear it. I figured it was better to mention it to the deputy first, rather than try to explain to Bob and Bart why they should tell the deputy their story, especially since they still didn't know that Avery Trowbridge was dead.

"Emma, it's your lead."

This time it was my partner who recalled my attention to the game. "Sorry," I said with a slight start. I scanned the cards in my hand and pulled the king of spades.

When the ace failed to appear, I led another spade, and my partner took the trick with the ace.

From that point I resolved to keep my mind on the game. When I had the opportunity to speak to Deputy Ainsworth again, I would inform him that Bob and Bart had something important to tell him. Besides, I needed the distraction that playing bridge always offered me. There would be time enough later to dwell on the murder.

By lunchtime we had played nine rubbers of bridge. We were all hungry by that point and ready to get up and stretch our legs. Sophie quickly added up the scores, and, not surprisingly, she and Bart won by a hefty margin. They had bid, and made, two small slams, and Bob and I never could catch up to them.

To my relief I had been able to concentrate on the game, and I kept the grim mental pictures of the murder scene at bay the whole time. I was determined to clear my mind for at least a while longer of what I had seen. I knew that if I let myself dwell on it, I wouldn't be able to eat a thing. Not that it wouldn't do me good to miss a few hundred calories, but I was beginning to feel a bit light-headed.

Bob and Bart excused themselves, and Sophie and I headed to the dining room.

"Are you going to tell Deputy Ainsworth what Bob and Bart told us?" Sophie asked me.

"I think I have to, don't you?" We paused at the entrance to the dining room and waited for someone to seat us. While we stood there, I spotted Marylou at a table with Paula.

I nudged Sophie. "There's Marylou over there, with Paula."

Sophie groaned inelegantly. "Do we have to sit with them? I'm not sure I can deal with Paula right now."

Marylou caught sight of us and waved.

"We don't have any choice now," I said, smiling and waving back. Trailed by a waitress with menus, we made our way over to their table and sat down. I was next to Paula, and Sophie was next to Marylou. The waitress said she would be back soon to take our order.

Marylou and Paula were already at the dessert

stage. Marylou seemed to be enjoying her chocolate mousse, but Paula was simply poking her fork in and out of a slice of pecan pie without eating any of it.

"How are you, Paula?" I asked. "I know this has all been such a terrible shock for you."

Sophie picked up a menu and hid her face behind it.

Paula picked at her dessert. For a moment I thought she wasn't going to answer, perhaps hadn't even heard me, but then she spoke. "I wanted to be rid of Avery, Lord knows, but not like this." She sighed, laying her fork aside. "He was a real shit, as it turned out, but I found out too late."

"Someone must have hated him pretty badly," Sophie said, closing her menu and placing it across her plate.

"They'd have to stand in line," Paula said. "He pissed off a lot of people lately."

"It's one thing to piss someone off," I said, "but it's something else again for one of those people to be angry enough to kill."

"You saw him in action," Paula said, looking at me, her eyes narrowed in speculation. "What do you think?"

"He was unpleasant," I admitted. "But I still say someone would have to have had a really strong motive to go to that length."

"You're right, Emma," Marylou said. "Now, Paula, you probably know everyone who had reason to hate Avery the most. Surely you have some idea of who might have killed him."

Paula glanced from one to the other of us. "What is this? You're beginning to sound like that deputy who was asking me so many questions."

"We can't help but be curious," Sophie said, shrugging. "I mean, it happened right next door to us. Plus we know you, and we met the victim. Wouldn't you be curious?"

"I suppose," Paula said, her tone grudging.

"So what do you say?" Marylou spoke again. "Who do you think did it?"

Paula glanced around as if to make sure no one could overhear what she was about to say. "Veronica, who else? She's a coldhearted bitch, and Avery humiliated her in public. I think she was really angry over what he did, plus the fact that he had no intention of continuing their affair."

"How do you know that?" I asked. "Or are you simply guessing?"

Paula stared at the remains of her pie. "Avery told me," she finally said. "I confronted him about it last night, and he told me he wasn't going to have anything more to do with her."

"When was this?" Marylou asked.

Paula shrugged. "I don't remember what time it was. Late, anyway. Avery was in a foul mood, and we argued. I told him I wanted a divorce, and he said it was fine with him."

"You must have been relieved to hear that," Sophie said. "Because didn't you tell us before that he was resisting?"

"What changed his mind?" I asked when Paula didn't respond right away to Sophie's question.

"I don't know why he changed his mind," Paula said, "and frankly I don't give a damn. I was just glad he finally agreed." She sighed heavily. "And now, of course, it's a moot point. He's dead."

A man's voice spoke then, startling us all. "He certainly is, and how convenient that is for you."

Chapter 15

Paula had picked up her water glass and was about to sip from it when the man spoke. She set the glass down with a loud thump, and water sloshed over the edge and onto the tablecloth.

"Haskell," Paula said. "What the *hell* are you talking about?" She glared up at the man who had come to a halt scant inches from our table.

Marylou, Sophie, and I stared at him. It took me a moment to remember who he was—Avery Trowbridge's agent. I had also forgotten how large he was. At the moment he loomed over us like a mountain.

Without being invited, he pulled a chair from a nearby table, twirled it around backward, and sat down with his arms across the back of it. He stared straight at Paula, ignoring the rest of us.

He laughed. "Come on, Paula, you're not fooling me one bit with this little outraged-innocence act. Avery told me he was going to divorce you, and he was going to see that you didn't get much out of the settlement." He paused for emphasis. "Now that he's dead, you stand to get a lot more than you would have otherwise."

For the first time he acknowledged the presence of

other persons at the table. "What do *you* think, ladies? Isn't it awfully *convenient* for Paula that somebody offs Avery before he can divorce her?"

"You had better be careful about saying such things," I said, "or Paula just might decide to sue you."

"I certainly will," Paula said in a fierce tone. "You had better shut your mouth, Haskell Crenshaw, or I'll hire somebody to shut it for you."

Crenshaw threw his hands up in a gesture of mock surrender. "Okay, okay, I give. So maybe Paula didn't kill Avery for the money." He laughed. "But it's still pretty convenient."

"It looked like a crime of passion to me," Paula said, her voice suddenly cool. "I didn't care enough about Avery to want to kill him. And I wasn't interested in his money. He was willing to give me a divorce, and that's all I cared about."

"She's very convincing, isn't she?" Crenshaw cocked his head at me.

"What are you playing at here?" I said. I couldn't take much more of this nasty little fencing match. "This is not a good place for this."

"Emma's right," Sophie said. "We've all had enough of these unpleasant public scenes." Marylou nodded in agreement.

"Sorry, ladies," Crenshaw said, though he didn't look in the least abashed. "But you can't tell me you really believe she's Little Miss Innocent in all this." He nodded at Paula.

"I have no idea what you're talking about," Paula said. "You're being ridiculous."

"Well, go ahead, Paula," Crenshaw said. "Let's have it. Tell us all about your little chat with Avery last night."

Paula stared hard at him for a moment. "You really think I don't know, don't you?" She shook her head, as if in sadness. "You really think Avery didn't talk to me about things, don't you?"

For the first time, Crenshaw appeared the slightest bit uneasy. He had been drumming his fingers on the back of the chair, but his hands stilled. His grip on the chair tightened as he waited for Paula to continue.

"For instance, Avery told me about how, every time you had a little too much to drink, you started trying to get him into your bed." Paula smiled, malice triumphant. "We had *so* many laughs about it, let me tell you. He thought you were *so* amusing. And *pathetic*, of course. The only reason he continued to put up with you was that he thought you were good at your job."

Crenshaw relaxed his grip on the back of the chair. Whatever he had been expecting, it wasn't this. He actually seemed relieved. In fact, he burst out laughing.

"What the hell is so funny?" Paula practically hissed at him.

It took Crenshaw a moment to stop laughing. "You really are as stupid as Avery said you are." He stared at her. "He lied to you, Paula. He was the one who wanted to get *me* into bed whenever he'd had a snootful. Ol' Avery traveled both sides of the street, if you get my drift."

"I don't believe you," Paula said, but without much conviction in her voice.

"Oh, you can believe it all right," Crenshaw said, his voice hardening. "You remember a few months ago, when Avery went to Acapulco for a week? He told you he was doing a bridge cruise, didn't he?"

Paula nodded. Her eyes narrowed.

"He was in Acapulco all right," Crenshaw said, "but it had nothing to do with bridge." He sighed as if he was recalling particularly happy memories. "We had a great time that week even though I had trouble getting Avery to leave our suite."

Paula was speechless for the moment, and I certainly couldn't think of anything to say. Sophie, Marylou, and I exchanged shocked glances.

At last Paula found her tongue. The words that came spewing out of her mouth were vile and vulgar. Marylou and I, after the first shock wore off, both reached for her at the same time. Paula's voice was rising in volume, and the few other diners nearby were staring at our table.

Through it all, Crenshaw just stared at Paula without appearing at all bothered by her words. As soon as Marylou and I managed to shut Paula up, however, he got up from his chair. "I think that's probably one reason Avery preferred my company to yours, Paula. You really are a shrew. It's been my pleasure, ladies," he said, sketching a slight bow. Then he turned and walked away.

"Maybe he's bluffing," Marylou said when he was out of the room. She patted Paula's arm in consoling fashion. "Don't let him upset you so."

"Marylou's right," Sophie said, and I nodded. "He's probably making all that up just to make you mad."

"I wish that was all there was to it," Paula said in a voice so low we could barely hear her.

"Do you mean to say that Avery really was bisexual?" Marylou's eyes grew round with surprise.

Paula nodded miserably. "That's one of the reasons I wanted to divorce him." A sob caught in her throat. "Oh, I could just die!" She started crying.

Marylou did her best to comfort Paula. Sophie and

I looked at each other. I knew we were both thinking the same thing.

If Paula had known about her husband's bisexuality, that could give her a motive for murder. She might have been so angry with him that she killed him, rather than simply divorcing him. I could imagine how I would feel after such a confession from my husband. Such promiscuity was unforgivable. •

"When did you find out about it, Paula?" I spoke gently. I thought at first she hadn't heard me, though her crying had quieted. She raised a tearstained face from Marylou's shoulder and regarded me blankly.

"When?" She wiped her face with one of the linen table napkins. "Last night, actually," she said. "He threw it in my face while we were arguing. I can't tell you how shocked I was." She paused for a deep, calming breath. "It makes me sick all over again just to think about it. I mean, I knew that he cheated on me with other women. But I never imagined, well, you know."

Her face crumpled, and she started to cry again. Marylou once again cradled Paula's head against her shoulder and did her best to offer comfort.

Sophie and I shook our heads at each other. Paula was too upset to realize how this would sound to the sheriff's department. A motive like this could make her their number one suspect right away.

And who was to say that Paula didn't kill him? I grimaced at Sophie. We knew each other so well we didn't have to speak to communicate sometimes.

What were we going to do about this?

If Paula was innocent, then she ought to have nothing to fear from telling all this to Deputy Ainsworth.

If she was guilty, then she would probably clinch her arrest by talking to the deputy about it.

Either way, the deputy would be mighty interested in this development. The question was, should we encourage Paula to talk to Ainsworth? Or should one of us talk to him and tell him?

I thought it would be better coming from Paula herself. If she didn't get to Ainsworth soon and tell him, I wouldn't put it past Haskell Crenshaw to do it himself. He seemed pretty intent on doing Paula as much damage as he could. If he really cared for Avery, he could be angry enough over what happened that he would tell the deputy everything.

"Come on, Paula," Marylou said, gently disentangling herself from her distraught friend. "I think we need to get you up to your room so you can wash your face and maybe lie down for a while. How does that sound?"

Paula nodded as she once again mopped her face with her sodden napkin. "I must look awful," she said, ducking her head. "My face gets so blotchy when I cry."

She was right about that. I felt so sorry for her, even though I was halfway to suspecting that she killed her husband.

"We'll go with you," Sophie said. She reached for our bill and quickly signed it and added our room number. Our waiter had dropped it off before the nasty little scene developed, thank goodness.

I trailed them out, aware of the eyes following us. Though no one had been sitting at a table right around us, there were people not too far away. They probably couldn't have helped overhearing some of what went on. All the more reason for Paula to talk to Ainsworth, and soon.

Haskell Crenshaw had managed to put Paula in a very difficult position, and I had no doubts that was what he intended. If he really cared for Avery, then he was probably hurting. He was leveling his anger at Paula as the wife of the man he had cared for, perhaps even loved.

Then I recalled the curious way he had reacted when Paula first confronted him about his alleged advances to her husband. He had been relieved rather than upset, almost as if he was expecting her to say something else.

That's when I remembered what I had overheard the day before, just outside Avery Trowbridge's door.

He had fired Haskell Crenshaw, he said, but Crenshaw was now acting as if it hadn't happened.

Why had Trowbridge fired him? To break off their personal relationship as well as their business one?

No matter what the answer, Haskell Crenshaw was in the same boat with Paula. A lover scorned had a powerful motive for murder.

Chapter 16

I kept all those thoughts to myself while we got Paula settled in her room. Marylou helped Paula wash her face and found some aspirin for her headache, then tucked her into bed. Paula smiled up gratefully at all of us. "Thank you for being so sweet to me," she said. "I know I'm being a pain, but right now you're the only friends I have. I just want you to know I appreciate how you're sticking by me."

Touched by her obvious sincerity, I felt a little uneasy over my earlier suspicions that she had killed Avery Trowbridge. I didn't think she was that good an actress. Someone that pathetically grateful for our kindnesses to her couldn't be a killer.

Could she?

I'd give myself a headache at this rate. Time enough later to think about Paula's possible guilt.

Sophie, Marylou, and I left Paula to get some rest. Out in the hall again, I turned to my friends. "Girls, do you remember what we overheard outside our room yesterday? I mean when Haskell Crenshaw tried to see Avery Trowbridge and got the door slammed in his face."

"Oh Lord, yes," Sophie said. "I can't believe I'd forgotten about that."

"I remembered," Marylou said. "I thought about bringing it up downstairs when he was accusing Paula. Should I have?"

"I don't know," I said. "Paula didn't seem to know about it. Don't you think?"

"I'm sure she would have said something about it if she did know," Sophie said.

"She certainly would have," Marylou said. "Probably Avery didn't have time to tell anyone he had fired Crenshaw except Crenshaw himself."

"Do you think we should talk to Ainsworth about this?" Sophie asked.

The elevator bell pinged right then, and the doors opened. Several people stepped out, leaving the car empty. I motioned for Marylou and Sophie to follow me into it. When they were safely inside, I punched the button for the ground floor.

"I think we probably should," I said.

"Do we all need to go?" Marylou asked.

I shook my head. "No, I'll do it. If he wants corroboration, he can always talk to you later."

"Good," Marylou said with obvious relief. "Then I think I'll go back to the ballroom and try to get in a few rubbers this afternoon. Sophie, how about you?"

"I'll come with you," Sophie said, eyeing me doubtfully.

"Sure, go ahead," I said. "I'll come along there as soon as I've spoken with the deputy."

The elevator halted at the ground floor, and we stepped out. Marylou and Sophie headed for the ballroom. My destination was the reception desk, to inquire where the sheriff's department personnel were based at the hotel.

When I reached the desk, the young girl, Veronica Hinkelmeier's daughter, was attempting to talk to a short, elderly man who was banging his fist on the counter. What was the girl's name? Monica, I saw when I glanced at the name badge she wore. I'd try to remember it from now on.

"I want to check out right now," the elderly man was saying.

"But, sir," Monica protested. Her voice was drowned out by the old man's increasingly loud complaints.

"Excuse me," I raised my voice over the din. Startled, the old man fell silent.

"What seems to be the problem here?" I asked in my normal voice.

Monica shot me a grateful glance before she replied. "Mr. Atwell wants to check out."

"This is a free country," Mr. Atwell said. "I should be able to leave this place when I damn well want to."

He appeared about to launch into his tirade again, but I caught his eye and glared down at him. This tactic worked most of the time.

Atwell spluttered to a halt, shooting me a baleful look.

"Why can't he leave?" I asked Monica.

"The sheriff's department said that nobody can leave the hotel right now," Monica said, rubbing her temples with trembling fingers. "I was trying to explain that to this gentleman, but he wouldn't listen."

I turned to Atwell. "If you have any complaints, sir, then I suggest you take them up with the sheriff's department. You heard the young lady. No one is allowed to leave right now." I glared at him again.

Atwell evidently decided that discretion was the better part of valor. He conceded the field and walked away, muttering under his breath.

"Wow," Monica said, a huge smile of relief on her face. "Thank you for helping me with him. I wish I could do that."

"Give it time," I said, smiling. "Just practice being more assertive. Don't let people like that bully you."

The girl straightened her shoulders a bit and gave me a huge grin. "What can I do for you?"

"Actually, I'm looking for the sheriff's-department people myself," I said. "Are they using a room here somewhere while they investigate?"

Monica nodded. "They're in the Alamo Room. It's in the other corridor. Not the one the ballroom is on, I mean." She pointed.

"Thanks, Monica," I said.

"No, thank *you*," she said, beaming.

I smiled as I turned away. She seemed like a very sweet girl. I didn't envy her having to deal with that mother of hers. Veronica Hinkelmeier seemed to belong to some species that devoured its young.

Following the signs and Monica's directions, I had little trouble locating the Alamo Room. Did every hotel in the state of Texas have an Alamo Room? I wondered idly. Shaking my head at such an inconsequential thought, I paused on the threshold of the open door.

Several persons in uniform occupied the room. Most of them were seated at tables scattered here and there. The hum of low-voiced conversations washed around me. Most of the officers were speaking on cell phones, some of them consulting notebooks or jotting things down in them. Deputy Ainsworth was talking on a cell phone, too, but when he caught sight of me, he motioned me toward him.

I approached the table where he sat, and took the

seat across from him, which he indicated with a brief smile and a tilt of his head. He concluded his conversation after a moment, then snapped his phone shut.

"Mrs. Diamond," he said. "Perfect timing. I was just about to send someone to find you, but you saved me the trouble." He smiled at me, but something in that smile made me wary.

"Oh, really," I said, feeling slightly flustered. "Well, here I am. I wanted to talk to you about something. What did you want to see *me* about?"

Again the deputy smiled at me, looking positively vulpine this time, and I shifted a bit in my chair. "You didn't tell me you were involved in another murder case, Mrs. Diamond. I find that very interesting about you."

How on earth had he found out so quickly?

I swallowed. "Um, well, it's not exactly the first thing you tell someone. And frankly, I didn't think it had any bearing on the present situation."

Ainsworth quirked an eyebrow at me. "You have to admit, it's quite a coincidence, you being on the scene of two murders, and only a few months apart."

"That's just what it is, coincidence," I said, my tone getting a bit testy. "Nothing more, I can assure you." I was itching to ask how he had found that out so quickly, but I was darned if I would ask him directly. He had probably been checking up on me, and Sophie and Marylou, with the Houston Police Department. "I'm sure Lieutenant Burnes in homicide at HPD would vouch for me."

"He did." Ainsworth had stopped smiling. "You found the body, Mrs. Diamond, and that automatically makes you a person of interest in this case. The fact that there are some special features to the case, well, you can see how I wanted to know everything I could."

Special features, meaning the queen of diamonds clutched in the dead man's hand. That was what he really meant but wouldn't say aloud.

I tried to maintain a calm demeanor as I replied. "Was Lieutenant Burnes able to assure you that I'm basically harmless?"

Ainsworth snorted with laughter. "That wasn't exactly the word he used to describe you." He eyed me critically for a moment. "Actually, he said you were kind of a busybody, but you were a helpful, smart busybody."

I didn't know whether to turn red from embarrassment or anger. Somehow I doubted that Burnes had spoken about me in such a patronizing manner. I started a slow burn.

The deputy must have read something in my face, because he suddenly turned conciliatory. "You have to understand my position, Mrs. Diamond. I have to look at all the angles, and right off the bat you interested me a lot. Now that I know a bit more about the situation, I can see that I was probably off base about you."

That was probably as much of an apology as I could expect to get from him. I decided to accept it, or appear, to anyway, although I wasn't convinced of its sincerity. "Thank you, Deputy," I said, trying to keep the frost out of my voice. The man was only doing his job, and he should have been suspicious of me, for the very reason he cited. But that didn't mean I had to like it.

"Burnes told me you and your friends basically solved the case for him," Ainsworth said, leaned back in his chair, and regarded me with a slight smile.

"That was very kind of him, though he was exaggerating," I told him. "We were only doing what we thought was right. We just shared whatever information we could with him." I winced inwardly. That sounded mealymouthed to me, because Sophie, Marylou, and I had very definitely been busybodies, sticking our noses into the murder investigation.

I doubted Ainsworth was fooled by my answer. I was sure that Lieutenant Burnes had given him an earful about the aging Nancy, Bess, and George who had interfered in his case.

"I'm still reserving my judgment about some things," Ainsworth said, with that eyebrow still raised. Then he relaxed it. "But I figure if you helped HPD, you can certainly help me and my team."

I eyed him carefully for a moment. Did he really mean that? Or was he being disingenuous on purpose? No matter what game he was playing, I decided I would go along with him. He would find out soon enough I was not the murderer.

"That's why I'm here," I said primly. "I have some things to tell you."

"Shoot," Ainsworth said.

It took me about ten minutes to tell him everything. I started with Bart and Bob and the mysterious phone call they had received, telling them the lesson was canceled. Ainsworth made a note of the men's names on a pad as I moved on to the bits involving Haskell Crenshaw.

The deputy's posture stiffened the more I talked about Avery Trowbridge's business manager and erstwhile lover and the sparring match Crenshaw had had with Paula.

When I finished, Ainsworth eyed me with fresh respect. "You certainly do manage to find things out."

I shrugged. "All this was purely accidental. I just happened to be in the right place at the right time, you might say."

Ainsworth nodded at that. "As long as you don't get yourself into any dangerous situations, I hope you're in more right places at the right times."

"Sharon McCone at your service," I said in a self-mocking tone.

"You read Marcia Muller?" Ainsworth said, surprising me a little.

"Yes," I said. "I read a lot of mysteries, and she's my favorite female PI writer."

"Mine, too," Ainsworth admitted. "Well, thank you, Mrs. Diamond. I have some new leads now, and I'm going to follow up on them." He rose from his chair, and I stood up, too. He stuck a hand across the table, and I shook hands with him.

"I think I'm going to play some bridge now," I said. Ainsworth nodded.

I left the Alamo Room feeling considerably relieved. Though I was still a bit embarrassed over it, I was glad that the deputy had spoken with Lieutenant Burnes. At least Sophie, Marylou, and I were off the list of suspects now, or pretty close to being taken off it. Ainsworth had also practically encouraged me to snoop around a bit as well. He seemed like a pretty sharp guy, and he was apparently willing to take what information he could get to help close this case.

I realized, with a certain amount of rue, he could be simply trying to catch me off guard by being so friendly.

Well, it really didn't matter. In the end, the truth would come out—and if Sophie, Marylou, and I helped bring the identity of the killer to light, that was fine with me.

I wandered down the corridor and through the lobby area, stopping to use the ladies' room. A few minutes later, at the doors of the ballroom, I paused to look around, hoping to spot Sophie and Marylou. This side of the ballroom was pretty full, with bridge games in progress at all the tables except four.

After a brief scan of the room I located Sophie and Marylou on the far side, near the partition between this section and the duplicate section. They were in the midst of a game when I drew closer to their table.

As I came to a halt a couple of feet away, I recognized one of the players—Lorraine Trowbridge. Then I recognized the other, her son, Will. This could be rather interesting.

"Emma, come and join us," Sophie said when she saw me. "Pull up one of those chairs." She pointed to an empty table nearby.

I brought a chair over to their table and placed it near Sophie. Sitting down, I greeted Marylou, Lorraine, and Will. Frankly I was a bit surprised to find them playing bridge. Surely they knew by now Avery had been murdered. I ventured a covert glance at Will.

He knew all right, and he was doing his best to appear calm. I could tell, though, that he was upset and probably wished he were somewhere else.

His mother, on the other hand, appeared perfectly serene and untroubled.

Sophie cut her eyes at me, and I braced myself.

"Emma," she said, "Lorraine's been telling us the most fascinating things about her ex-husband's will."

I winced. Sophie was never this tactless unless she meant to be. What was she trying to do?

"I don't feel like playing anymore," Will Trowbridge said. He stood up and dropped his cards face-down on the table. "Excuse me." He stared at his mother for a moment, with something close to loathing on his face. Then he left, almost running from the room.

Chapter 17

I stared after the fleeing Will, half tempted to go after him. He looked very upset, and it quickly became obvious that his mother wasn't too concerned about him.

Sophie caught my eye and grimaced slightly. I could tell she regretted upsetting Will, but evidently she had a good reason for the remark.

"He'll be perfectly fine," Lorraine Trowbridge said, offering a wintry smile to Sophie, Marylou, and me. "Naturally he's upset, although he and his father have never been very close. I would go after him, but I know he'd rather be on his own for a while." She gestured with one hand. "Why don't you take Will's place?"

I supposed, in this case, mother knew best, but I still thought the woman was being extremely casual about her son's distress. I forbore saying anything, however. I moved from my chair to the one Will had vacated, and picked up his cards.

Sophie and I were partners, and Marylou had the dummy hand.

"What are we playing?" I asked.

"The contract is three spades," Sophie replied. "We've gone only one round in this game." She picked up the cards in front of her and showed them to me—the ace, king, jack, and three of hearts. "I led with the jack. Lorraine played the king from the board. Your hand took the trick with the ace of hearts."

Now it was my lead. I took a moment to examine my hand. I had two hearts left, the queen and the ten—two potentially good tricks. In addition I held four small spades, three loser diamonds, and three clubs, including the ace. I wondered whether Lorraine would follow up on Sophie's provocative remark about Avery's will. For the moment, though, Lorraine seemed intent on the game. Maybe she would talk once play was under way. If not, I was sure Sophie would try to goad her into it again.

I returned my partner's lead by playing the queen of hearts. Lorraine played the four from her hand, Sophie dumped a loser club, and Lorraine pulled the six from dummy's hand. Sophie collected the trick while I pondered my lead. Should I play my ten of hearts? Seven hearts had dropped so far, and my ten made eight. That meant there were still five out. There were three on the board.

Pulling the ten of hearts from my hand, I dropped it on the table. Once that round was done, Lorraine held the high heart in her hand. If I'd had another heart to lead back for Sophie to trump, we would have had another easy trick.

So far Lorraine hadn't said a word, instead concentrating on the game. One of us would have to get her to talking, I supposed, but I decided not to say anything until the hand was done.

Remembering that Sophie had sloughed a club on my queen of hearts, I played my ace. Everyone followed suit, but Sophie played the ten. I led with my remaining club, and Sophie played the king. Since both Lorraine and dummy followed suit, we won that trick, giving us five. Lorraine and Marylou were already down one.

That was the last trick we took, however. Lorraine got in with the next round, when Sophie led the queen of clubs. I played my remaining club, and dummy contributed its last one, the ten. Lorraine trumped with the two of spades. I glanced at Sophie, who shrugged slightly. She held the five remaining clubs, including the jack, but they were useless by that point.

Once Lorraine was in, she pulled trump. The rest of the tricks were hers, but she was still one down. "That was unpleasant," she said, laughing a little.

"If the lead had been different," I said in tones of sympathy, "you probably would have made it just fine. We were just lucky with the hearts and the clubs. You could have sloughed a loser heart or a club on your good diamonds."

Lorraine nodded, but she didn't appear in the least interested in my analysis.

Marylou noted the score before picking up the cards to deal. As the cards dropped in front of us, I looked at Lorraine, my head tilted to one side. "So what was it Sophie was saying when I first came up? Something about your late husband's will?" If Sophie wasn't going to ask, I might as well. There had to be a point to all this besides getting Will out of the room.

There was no way to make that sound anything but nosy, but Lorraine didn't seem bothered by my obvious interest.

"It's really quite interesting," Sophie said.

"I suppose, but it's not really Avery's will I was talking about. It was his father's," Lorraine said. "I don't pretend to understand all the ins and outs of all this legal stuff." She shrugged, a gesture no doubt meant to indicate that she had no interest in "legal stuff." She picked up her cards and began to arrange them. For a moment I thought she wasn't going to say anything else, but she continued, somewhat abruptly.

"Avery's father made a fortune in something to do with the oil business," she said while staring at her cards. "He had more money than he knew what to do with, but he knew that Avery couldn't handle it. He'd have gone broke in two years after his father died if the old man hadn't tied it up so he couldn't get his hands on most of it."

"Really," I said. "That must have been frustrating for Avery, though."

Lorraine grinned. "Drove him absolutely mad, but there was nothing he could do about it. He tried to contest the will, but nothing doing. The old man was perfectly sane when he did it."

"So Avery never got anything from his father's fortune?" I asked.

"Oh, he had a very nice income from a trust fund his father set up after Avery and I married," Lorraine said. "But the old man made sure Avery would never be able to touch the bulk of his money. Instead, he stipulated in his will that control of the money would go to his grandson, when Will turns twenty-five." She smiled briefly. "Will turns twenty-one in March, so it will be a while before he comes into it."

"What happens to Avery's trust fund?" I couldn't stop myself. Lorraine didn't appear to mind spilling the beans, so to speak, and Sophie and Marylou were just as curious as I was.

"I'm not really sure," Lorraine said. "I don't know whether he was able to will it to anyone. There might be something in the old man's will about it." She shrugged. "I'm sure the lawyers will get it all sorted out."

"I'm sure they will," Marylou said. "They always do."

"Yes," Lorraine said. "Now, who dealt? Whose bid is it?"

"Mine," Marylou said, taking the hint. Obviously Lorraine had said all she was going to say about wills.

We finished the rubber. Lorraine didn't offer any more details about Avery or his will, and the rest of us refrained from prodding her for them. Once the rubber was done, Lorraine declared she was going to her room for a rest. We said good-bye, waiting until she was out of earshot before we discussed what she had told us.

"I'm not quite sure I trust her," I said.

"What do you mean?" Marylou asked.

"I bet she means that Lorraine was probably lying about what happens to Avery's trust fund," Sophie said, smiling at me. "Right, Emma?" I nodded at her, and she went on. "She didn't fool me for a minute. I bet you she knows everything there is to know about what happens to the money in that family."

"Exactly," I said. "She impresses me as the kind of woman who knows whatever she needs to know about money. The way she dresses, she obviously has expensive tastes. That was a designer dress she was wearing—Vera Wang, if I'm not mistaken."

Sophie hooted with laughter. "Emma, I don't believe it. You're right. Since when do you know how to recognize designer work?"

"Maybe because you keep rubbing my nose in the fact that I'm illiterate when it comes to haute couture," I said. "I've been trying to learn a bit about it so you can't be so superior all the time." I grinned at her, and she stuck her tongue out at me.

Marylou was laughing, and Sophie and I began to chuckle as well. When we stopped, Marylou said, "I think y'all are right. Lorraine is too shrewd not to know about the money. She lied to us about that."

"The question is, why?" I said. "She didn't have to tell us any of that, but she did. Why was she so coy about that one thing?"

"Because the truth about it might reveal that she had a good motive to kill Avery," Sophie said.

I nodded. "That's what I was thinking. But of course we could never get her to admit that." I pushed back from the table. "I don't know about you two, but I need to do something to clear my head a little. The weather is nice today, and I thought I might take a walk around the grounds. Why don't you come with me?" I looked to each of them in turn.

Sophie rolled her eyes at me.

"Well, it was worth a shot," I said. "I should have known the mention of exercise would put you off. So what are you going to do?"

"Play some more bridge," she said. "Marylou? Are you game?"

Marylou nodded at her, then turned to me with a slightly sheepish grin. "Sorry, Emma."

"It's okay," I said. "I'll feel even more virtuous if you two stay here." I waggled my fingers at them before I turned and headed for the door of the ballroom.

I could have stayed and played bridge with them, but I really wanted to get away from everything and everyone for a little while. I loved my friends dearly, but every once in a while, we each needed time on our own. I certainly could use the exercise as well, I noted ruefully as I glanced down at my waistline.

Once I reached the veranda at the front of the hotel, I stood there for a few moments, shading my eyes against the bright sunlight. I had a small handbag with me, and I looked inside it to see whether I had stuck my sunglasses in it.

Ah, there they were. I slipped them on, and my eyes felt better immediately. Now I could leave the veranda and walk around in the sun.

There were several marked paths, and I started following one that seemed to lead in the direction of the woods, not too far away. I thought it might be pleasant to wander among the trees for a little while, so I quickened my pace slightly now that I had a specific goal.

Looking ahead, I spotted a bench near the path, about halfway between me and the trees. The bench was occupied by one person, a man with his back to me. Something about the back of the figure seemed familiar, but I couldn't determine why. While I stared at the man's back, willing him to turn so I could see his face, I saw instead the smoke of a cigarette spiraling over his head.

Finally, when I was about only a dozen or so feet away, I recognized the man. Or perhaps I should say "the boy." It was Will Trowbridge. He might be almost twenty-one, but he seemed more like a boy to me.

Hearing my approach, Will turned a slightly sullen face in my direction. He took another drag on his cigarette, exhaling smoke, before he turned away again.

I know I should have minded my own business, but there was something in his posture that affected me. He seemed so forlorn, and yet defiant, at the same time. I decided to try to talk to him, if he would let me.

"Hi, Will," I said as I reached the bench. I stopped

near him. "Do you mind if I sit down for a moment or two?"

He shrugged. "Whatever." He held up his cigarette. "This bother you?"

"No," I said. "Go ahead." I didn't want to antagonize him, and fortunately there was a breeze to waft the smoke away from me.

My response elicited a brief smile, and I took that as encouragement.

"You know, I can't remember if we were ever properly introduced. I'm Emma Diamond." I said.

He nodded, his cigarette dangling from his mouth. "I know. Will Trowbridge." He stuck out a hand.

I shook his hand. "Thanks, Will." He released my hand, and we regarded each other in silence.

"I'm very sorry about your father," I said.

He tensed, and for a moment I thought he was going to get up and walk away. "Thanks," he said, his voice suddenly gruff.

Again there was silence. I waited.

Will spoke after a minute or two. "So what did my mother tell you about the will?"

I figured I had better be very careful here. Ill-chosen words on my part might cause further tension between Will and his mother, and I definitely did not want that. Her willingness to talk about intimate family matters to strangers had obviously bothered him enough to make him leave the room. I wondered idly how long he had been out here. Glancing at the grass around his feet, I counted seven cigarette butts.

"Oh," I said, trying to be as nonchalant as possible, "she just told us some general things. About your grandfather's will and so on, and your father's trust fund."

Will dropped his cigarette on the grass and ground it fiercely with the heel of his shoe. "I'll just bet she did," he muttered.

"I'm sorry, Will," I said, partly to fill the awkward pause that followed his words, but mostly because I really did have great sympathy for him. "I know none of it is really any of my business."

"Not your fault," he said, shrugging. "My mother makes it everyone's business. God knows why, but she does."

I didn't answer that. Frankly, I wasn't sure what to say to him at that point.

He didn't seem to notice my silence. He turned to face me after a moment. "Just what *did* she say about my father's trust fund?"

I struggled for the words to put it as diplomatically as possible. "I believe she said she wasn't sure what would happen to it, now that your father is . . . gone."

He snorted in disbelief. "I can't believe she's pulling that shit." He had the grace to look slightly abashed. "Sorry."

I waved his apology away. I had certainly heard worse in the classroom.

"Why do you say that?" I asked.

"Because she knows damn well what happens to that trust fund," Will said, his face reddening in anger. "It's hers now, for the rest of her life." His shoulders slumped, and he stared at me, misery replacing the anger.

He didn't have to put into words what he was thinking—what he feared, rather. He knew as well as I did that the trust fund gave his mother a very good motive for murder.

Chapter 18

I thought carefully for a moment before replying. "I'm sure your mother is upset by all that's happened, and she's probably not thinking very clearly."

Will grunted. He pulled a cigarette packet out of his shirt pocket, shook it, and then crumpled it in his hand when he discovered it was empty. He tossed it into a trash can nearby.

"Good shot," I said, knowing it probably sounded fatuous, but wanting to do something to break the silence.

"Thanks," he said. He put his hands on his knees, his shoulders slumping a bit. He turned his head to look at me for a moment. Then he shifted to stare out into the woods ahead of us. "Look, I don't want you to get the wrong impression. I love my mother. It hasn't always been very easy for her because of my dad. He, well, he wasn't always around when he should have been while I was growing up."

"I know what that's like," I said. "Neither of my parents was around very much when my brother and I were growing up. We had nannies and servants around us all the time. They were the ones who really took care of us."

"Seriously?" Will sat up and looked at me with open curiosity.

I nodded. "I wish it had been different. Sometimes I think I would give anything to have ordinary parents, but they weren't. They were who they were, or rather, they are who they are."

"They're both still around?"

"Yes, but I hardly ever see them. They spend a lot of time traveling, and when they're in Houston, they're usually so busy they don't have much time for my brother and me."

"That's pretty shitty," Will said, and this time he didn't apologize.

"It is," I agreed. "The point is, my brother and I managed to get on with our lives, and I think we both turned out pretty well, despite the way our parents are."

Will thought about that for a moment. "When I was little, things weren't so bad. My parents actually used to get along then, but when I was about twelve, it all just started going wrong." He stopped and looked at me again.

"You don't have to go into details," I said. "I have some idea of what went wrong." I turned my head away to stare off into the distance. "I know your father's second wife, for one thing."

"Paula."

There was much to read in his voice from that one word.

"Yes," I said. "I only met Paula recently. It turns out that she's an old friend of a friend of mine."

"I never could figure out why my dad married her," Will said. He sat back on the bench and folded his arms across his chest. "Maybe because she was too dumb to catch on to what he was doing, and he thought he could have it both ways. If you know what I mean?" He arched an eyebrow in my direction.

Feeling just a bit embarrassed, I nodded.

"Mom almost had a stroke when she found out," Will said. "That's when she divorced him."

"Will, do you mind if I ask you something?" I said.

He shrugged. "Sure, go ahead."

"Why on earth did your father marry again? It seems to me he would have been better off staying single."

Will responded with a snort of disgust. "That's what he should have done. But he had an *image* to protect in the bridge world. It's no big thing to get a divorce, but if word had gotten out just why he and my mom divorced, well . . ." He gestured with one hand, his thumb pointed downward.

"I see what you mean," I said, and I did. Paula had been an important part of Avery's facade of respectability.

" 'Oh what a tangled web we weave,' " Will quoted. He cut his eyes sideways at me in an interrogative manner.

" 'When first we practise to deceive,' " I said, capping the quotation. "Canto six of 'Marmion' by Sir Walter Scott."

"So, do you teach English?" Will asked with a smile.

"History," I said without thinking. Then I had to laugh. "How did you know I was a teacher?"

Will laughed with me. "Just a guess."

"A very astute one."

He blushed a little. "Thanks." He stood up. "I guess I'd better go back. Mom will be wondering where I am." He hesitated a moment. "And thanks for listening."

I looked up into his face. He was still just a boy in many ways, but there was an all-too-adult weariness in his eyes. "You're welcome, Will," I said. "And if you should need to talk again, well, I'll be happy to, whenever you like."

He nodded and gave me a shy smile.

I watched him as he walked away, his shoulders slumped. He seemed like a bright, personable young man, and he had certainly had to bear some things no child or adolescent should have to endure. He was troubled about his father's death, and at some level, he was probably grieving for the man. He didn't seem ready to talk about that, though, and I probably wasn't the best person for him to use as a therapist.

With a troubled sigh, I turned to face the trees again. My heart went out to Will, but I couldn't let sympathy cloud my reasoning too much. Will might very well be a nice young man, but other seemingly nice young men had turned out to be killers. Will could finally have had enough of his father's behavior and snapped.

I didn't really want to believe Will could be the murderer, but I couldn't ignore the possibility.

Time to walk again, I decided. Getting up from the bench, I followed the trail toward the trees. Perhaps physical activity would help clear my head and allow me to see things more objectively.

Removing my sunglasses and stowing them in my bag, I stepped into the woods. The trail appeared to be well defined, so I ought not get lost if I stuck to it. I had no idea where the trail led, but I could turn back whenever I wanted.

The woods were cool and shady. I hadn't realized quite how warm I had been, sitting on that bench in the direct sunlight. At the moment, the trees and the undergrowth weren't too thick, but the farther I walked along the trail, the denser the woods became. Trees stood much closer together here, and the light filtering from above was murky. I could see just well enough to know where I was going and, more importantly, watch out for snakes.

My mind turned irresistibly back to the murder. Who could have done it?

My first choice was Veronica Hinkelmeier. That was based as much on my intense dislike of her as anything else. The woman was a first-class bitch. I usually didn't like to use that term to refer to another woman, but I figured that, this once at least, it was all too apt. She definitely appeared to have the temperament, and Avery Trowbridge had humiliated her in public.

Plus, thanks to what Haskell Crenshaw had revealed, there was another possible motive. I doubted Veronica would have taken the news of Avery's bisexuality lightly. My question now was whether she had known.

I thought about it a moment, but I couldn't come up with a way to find out, other than by simply asking her outright. Of course, Deputy Ainsworth would probably be asking her that. Too bad I couldn't sit in on that interview.

Something moved nearby, and I stopped suddenly, my heart pounding. Standing completely still, I peered into the gloom around me, trying to identify the source of the sounds.

Then I saw it. About six or seven yards away from me, standing in a small clearing, were a doe and her fawn. They stared at me for a moment before quickly bounding away.

Charmed by the sight, and relieved as well, I could feel my heart settling back to its normal rate. I took a deep breath and continued on my walk.

Where was I? Veronica, I reminded myself. She was a good candidate for murder, a *crime passionnel,* as the French would say. She was passionate, if anything.

Lorraine Trowbridge had a monetary motive, if what Will had told me was true. With Avery's death, she inherited the trust fund her father-in-law had set up. I had no idea how much money that was, but it had to be fairly substantial if Will's grandfather had been as rich as Lorraine claimed. Of course, Lorraine could have done it simply out of hatred, I supposed. The money was a bonus.

But in that case, why would she wait so long to do it?

No, I decided, the financial motive was more probable in Lorraine's case. I wondered if Will could, or would, tell me how much money was involved. Then I had to laugh. I was turning into a real busybody if I thought I could ask people such things and get an answer.

Who else, then, besides Veronica and Lorraine?

There was Haskell Crenshaw. Avery had fired him as a business manager and an agent, and more than likely as a lover, too. Another case of a *crime passionnel,* I mused, but had Crenshaw been in love with his client? When he had spilled the beans to Paula, I had a hard time reading him. It might have been jealousy making him act that way. But I wasn't too sure about that.

In Crenshaw's case, the motive was far more likely financial. If Avery had fired him as a business manager, he might have had a good reason, other than simply tiring of the more personal side of their relationship. What if Crenshaw had been embezzling from Avery, and Avery threatened to take action?

It was at least plausible, I reckoned.

Now I came to Paula. I had mixed feelings about her. She often irritated the heck out of me, but sometimes she did arouse a kinder response. She had been angry with her husband, but had she been angry enough to kill him?

I heard a sound somewhere nearby, and I halted to scan the underbrush. The sound came again, and now I realized it came from behind me.

Just as I began to turn, something hit my back with considerable force. I stumbled and went down hard. Then everything went dark.

Chapter 19

"Emma! Emma, wake up!"

Dimly I heard a voice calling to me. Then I felt someone's hands on my arms.

"Emma, please."

Sophie's voice, sounding upset, penetrated through the fog in my head.

I opened my eyes, and there she was, looming over me.

"Sophie," I said as I tried to sit up. That hurt. "Ow," I said.

"Did you hit your head?" Sophie asked. "Maybe you should lie still."

"No, it's not my head," I said, continuing the struggle to sit up. Sophie slipped an arm around my shoulders to help. "No, it's actually my back that hurts."

"So you didn't hit your head?"

"I might have," I said, putting my hands up to feel around on my head, now that I was sitting up. I found a small bump on the back of my head. Fortunately for me, my hair is really thick, so the impact had been cushioned, even though I had blacked out.

"Maybe you hit this log," Sophie said.

I turned my head a bit. "Yes, you're probably right. But something struck me, hard, and that's what made me fall."

"Can you sit up by yourself?"

"Yes," I said.

Sophie released me and stood up. She examined the trail around us, then started poking with a long, thick branch into the underbrush on either side.

I watched her idly for a moment, trying to gather my wits. I still felt a bit dazed.

"How did you happen to find me?" I asked.

"I decided I wanted some fresh air, just to get away from the bridge table for a little while," Sophie said, "and I decided to come looking for you. It's a good thing I did."

She stopped poking with the branch and stared down at something about six feet away from where I sat. "There's a really big rock here, and it looks to me like somebody dropped it here recently." She bent down for a closer look. "I bet it weighs about ten pounds. Something like that thrown at you could certainly knock you over."

"Come help me up," I said, reaching out a hand.

"Are you sure you're ready? Maybe you should sit there a little bit longer." Sophie came over to me, but she didn't offer to help me up.

"Yes, I'm ready. This ground is cold and a little bit damp. I'll be okay," I said.

"All right." Sophie dropped the branch and took hold of my hands. With her aid I got to my feet, though I was a bit wobbly for a moment.

"Okay?" Sophie asked.

"Yes. My back is stiff from that cold ground, and from the rock someone threw at me. But a hot shower will help."

"What about your head?" Sophie said. "I'm afraid you might have a concussion."

"I don't think so," I said, thinking about it for a moment. "My head is clear now, and my vision is fine. The back of my head is a bit sore, but I don't have a headache or anything."

"You blacked out, didn't you?"

"Yes, but I don't know for how long."

"Then you need to see a doctor," Sophie said. "I'm going to get you back to the hotel, and we'll see about having your head examined."

I couldn't help laughing at that.

"Emma, you know what I meant," Sophie said, sounding exasperated.

"I know," I said, "but it just struck me as funny."

"Come on," Sophie replied. She slipped an arm around my waist. "Let's go back to the hotel."

"Where's my purse?" Suddenly I remembered that I'd had a bag with me.

"Right here," Sophie said. Releasing me for a moment, she stepped a pace away and bent down to pick up my bag. Straightening, she handed it to me. "You should probably check to see if anything has been taken."

"Let's get out of these woods first," I said. "It's getting cooler in here, and I want to feel some warm sunshine."

"Of course," Sophie said. Once more she put her arm around me, and off we went.

We reached the edge of the woods about seven or eight minutes later. I had gone farther along the trail into the woods than I had realized.

I stood blinking in the sunlight for a moment while my eyes adjusted. My vision was clear, and my eyes didn't seem to be unduly sensitive to the light. I opened my bag and rummaged for my sunglasses. Once I had them on, I examined the contents of the bag more carefully while Sophie watched.

"Looks like everything's here," I said. "All my credit cards, my cash, everything."

"Okay," Sophie said. "Then let's get back to the hotel and see about that doctor."

Slowly we made our way back to the hotel. My back would probably be stiff as all get-out by tonight, but I hoped that would be the worst of it.

"Why did someone throw that big rock at me?" I asked. "And who was it?"

"I was wondering the same things myself," Sophie admitted. "But I didn't want to say anything, in case you didn't want to talk about it right now."

"If someone wasn't trying to rob me," I said, "then why?"

"Maybe someone's angry with you."

"I guess so," I said. "But who could I have made angry?"

Sophie snorted with laughter. "Well, Veronica Hinkelmeier, for one. You told her how the cow ate the cabbage yesterday, didn't you?"

"Yes, I guess I did," I said, recalling the scene in the dining room when Veronica had tried to embarrass Paula over her credit card.

"She strikes me as someone who's probably vindictive," Sophie said.

"She struck me the same way," I said, then laughed at the unintentional pun. Sophie joined in.

"Seriously, though," Sophie said after a moment. "Who else could it be? Is there anyone else you've had a run-in with?"

"No," I said. "Unless someone is trying to warn me off from being nosy. Gosh, I feel just like Nancy Drew. She got hit on the head a few times, didn't she?"

"Yes, she did, but don't you start making a habit of it," Sophie said in a wry tone.

I thought of an important question. "Did you see anyone out here when you came looking for me?"

"No," Sophie said. "There wasn't anyone on the grounds when I walked across to the woods. I figured you might be walking through the woods, so I came straight to them. There wasn't anyone in the woods either."

By now we were approaching the front of the hotel. I paused on the veranda to remove my sunglasses and stick them in my bag. Sophie opened the door for us, and I preceded her inside. Still shepherding me along, she headed for the reception desk.

Monica was on duty, and her eyes widened with pleasure when she saw me. "Good afternoon, ladies. What can I do for you?"

"Do you have a doctor on call for the hotel?" Sophie was brisk, but polite.

"Yes, ma'am," Monica said, startled. "Is one of you sick?"

"Mrs. Diamond fell in the woods"—Sophie cut her eyes sideways at me, and I gave a slight nod—"and I think she ought to have a doctor look at her and make sure everything's okay."

Her eyes full of concern, Monica stared at me a moment. "I'll call the doctor right away. Is it an emergency?"

"No, probably not an emergency," Sophie said, "but I think she should be seen very soon. Just in case she might have a concussion."

Monica nodded. "I'll call now. Why don't you go on up to your suite and rest until the doctor arrives? Is there anything else I can do for you, or get for you?"

"No, not at the moment," Sophie said.

"Thank you, Monica," I said, smiling at her.

She returned the smile as she reached for the phone. We left her punching in the number and made our way to the elevator.

Marylou was evidently still playing bridge. Our suite was empty.

"I'm going to take a hot shower," I said as Sophie escorted me into the bedroom.

"How's your head?" Sophie asked as I dropped my bag on the bed.

"It's okay," I said. "My head is clear. It's just my back that's bothering me a little."

"Okay, then," Sophie said. "But I'm going to pull a chair up close to the bathroom door. You call out if you need anything."

"I wouldn't mind some water before I get in the shower," I said, and almost before the words were out of my mouth, Sophie found me a bottle of water and opened it.

"Thanks," I said, then drank about half the bottle.

Sophie took it from me when I headed toward the bathroom. She was watching me anxiously. "I'll be just fine," I said. "I wouldn't mind some hot tea when I get out of the shower."

"Right," Sophie said. I knew that giving her at least one little task would make her feel better.

I slipped into the bathroom, leaving the door slightly ajar. I knew better than to argue with Sophie about her monitoring me while I showered.

The hot water felt wonderful on my back. The

showerhead adjusted to several settings, and I experimented until I found the one I liked best. Then I stood there and let the water beat down on me.

While I enjoyed the shower, I thought back over what I had been doing just before I was hit by the rock.

I had been mulling over the different suspects in the murder. I had reached Paula when I heard a sound from behind me on the trail.

That's when I was struck by the rock and went down.

The fact that I could recall what happened immediately before I blacked out was a good sign, I knew. I figured the doctor would examine me and say that I just needed to rest for several hours and stay awake. I would have to be aware of the symptoms of concussion, though, because some of them could occur later.

I was a bit surprised that I had blacked out. The only other time I could remember fainting was the night when the police came to tell me that my husband had been killed in an accident on the Gulf Freeway in Houston. Recalling that, I felt the tears threatening to stream down my face. I steadied myself mentally. Now was not a good time to get upset.

I wasn't aware how long I was in the shower, but I heard Sophie calling me. I slid the shower door open a bit and stuck my head out. "Yes?"

"The doctor's here, Emma," Sophie said.

"Be right out." I shut off the water and stood there for a moment, dripping. The doctor had responded quickly, or else I had been in the shower a lot longer than I thought.

Stepping out of the shower, I reached for one of the luxurious hotel towels and dried myself off.

I emerged from the shower a few minutes later,

wearing one of the hotel robes, a lush terry-cloth affair that hung past my knees. Sophie had appropriated the smaller one, but I didn't mind. This one suited my purposes just fine.

Sophie introduced me to a rather nondescript man in his mid-sixties and explained that he had been en route to the hotel when Monica's call came. Apparently one of the elderly guests had suffered an attack of gout, and someone had already called Dr. McKenzie to attend.

"Thank you for coming, Dr. McKenzie," I said. "I think I'm probably okay, but I guess it's best to check."

Though plain, his face had a kindly expression. "Your friend told me you tripped over something in the woods and hit your head when you fell."

"Um, yes, that's more or less what happened," I said. For a moment I was baffled; then I realized Sophie was right not to broadcast that I had been attacked by an unknown assailant.

"Right, then, let's have a look at you," the doctor said. Setting his bag down on the bed, he motioned for me to have a seat in the chair Sophie had pulled up for me.

In the next several minutes he examined me carefully and asked me numerous questions. When he finished, he studied me for a moment before speaking.

"The fact that you blacked out, even briefly, concerns me, but all the signs are good otherwise." He frowned. "I'd like you to stay awake as long as possible, say until midnight. Take it easy, and no stimulants or depressants."

"In other words, no caffeine or alcohol," I said, smiling.

"A little caffeine perhaps," he said. "Some hot tea

would be fine. A light meal this evening. If you feel light-headed or have blurry vision, headaches, nausea, or anything like that in the next few days, call me at once."

"Thank you, Dr. McKenzie," I said, and Sophie added her thanks. She saw him out, and when she came back, she found me tucked up in my bed.

"I'll have your tea for you in a minute," Sophie said. "I'm surprised you didn't argue with the doctor and try to get up and do things."

"I may have got a bump on the head like Nancy Drew, but unlike her, I'm not a perennial teenager. I know good advice when I hear it."

"Good," Sophie said as she fussed over the tea things on a table near the bathroom. "I'm glad you're being sensible." Moments later she brought me my tea, with milk and sugar.

I sipped at it gratefully. *"Merci beaucoup."*

"De rien," Sophie responded. "The doctor said you should stay awake. What shall we do to keep you awake?"

"Canasta," I said. "I brought some cards. They're in my bag in the closet. Let's play for a while."

Sophie retrieved two decks of cards, then found a pencil and some paper, and we settled down to play.

Marylou appeared around six thirty, startled to find me in bed. Sophie explained what had happened to me, and Marylou fussed over me for a few minutes. Finally I was able to reassure her enough that she agreed to go down to dinner and then on to more bridge as she had planned.

"I'll stay with Emma," Sophie said. "You go on."

"If you're sure," Marylou said, hesitating in the doorway of our room.

"I'm going to throw something at you if you don't go on," I said, pretending to look around.

"I'm gone," Marylou said, throwing up her hands in surrender before she disappeared.

"She's such a dear," Sophie said. "I wonder what it would have been like to have Marylou for a mother."

"I think we do," I said, smiling at her.

"You're right," Sophie said, giggling.

We played canasta until nearly midnight, taking a break only when the food we had ordered from room service was delivered. Marylou came in at one. I was still awake, but Sophie had dozed off on her bed, fully clothed.

Marylou tiptoed into the room. "How are you?" she whispered.

"I'm fine," I said. "I think I'm going to go to sleep now, though."

Nodding, Marylou approached Sophie and gently shook her awake. Sophie sat up on the side of the bed and stared blankly at us for a moment.

"Time for bed," I said.

"Are you sure?" Sophie asked, alert at once.

"I'm fine," I said. "My head is perfectly clear, no headache, only a little stiffness in my back. We all need to get some sleep."

"Well, good night, then." Marylou came over to my bed, bent down, and kissed my forehead. "Sleep well, Emma, dear."

"Thank you," I said. "You, too."

Sophie and Marylou bade each other good night. I slid down in my bed and got comfortable while Sophie changed into a nightgown.

"G'night," she said, and in moments she was sound asleep again.

Not for the first time, I envied her that quick ability to fall asleep. I was tired, but my mind wasn't quite ready for sleep yet.

As I lay there, courting sleep by trying to still my mind, I suddenly realized that I had never told Sophie or Marylou about my conversation with Will Trowbridge. That could wait until morning, of course.

Determined to fall asleep, I concentrated on emptying my mind. There shouldn't be any voices coming through the air vent this time to disturb me. I shivered, then scolded myself for thinking about that.

Relax, I told myself sternly. Gradually, I slipped into a dreamy state, and finally into sound sleep.

Chapter 20

The next morning I felt fine except for the same stiffness in my back. A hot shower would help that. I felt on my head for the bump I'd had yesterday, but it appeared to have gone down, leaving only a small tender spot in its place. Otherwise my head felt just fine, too, so I wasn't particularly worried about the possible concussion.

Swinging my feet out of bed and onto the floor, I stood up—again, no problems. I glanced over at Sophie, who was still sound asleep. Then my eyes wandered to the clock. It was a few minutes past eight.

Before getting into the shower, I started the coffee. I wanted some caffeine, and then I wanted some breakfast. To my surprise, I was quite hungry. That had to be a good sign. I smiled as I stepped into the shower.

Twenty minutes later I was out of the shower and dressed, makeup done, sitting on the side of my bed. Sophie had woken while I was in the shower, and now she occupied the bathroom while I sipped at my coffee. I was debating whether to go to Marylou's room when a light knock sounded on our door.

"Come in," I called, and the door opened.

"Good morning, Emma," Marylou said. She was fully dressed and no doubt ready for breakfast, just as I was. "How are you feeling?"

"I'm fine," I said. "Just a little stiffness when I woke up, but another hot shower helped tremendously." I got up from the bed as I spoke and walked toward Marylou.

"I'm so glad," Marylou said. "What an awful thing for someone to do." She stood aside for me to pass by, then followed me into the living room.

We sat down on the sofa, and I continued to sip at my coffee.

Marylou regarded me with curiosity. "Why do you think they did it?"

I shrugged. "Who knows? I must have annoyed someone by doing something, I suppose." I laughed. "My best guess is Veronica Hinkelmeier because of the way I told her off the other day."

"Sounds like something she would do," Marylou said. "She is *such* an unpleasant person."

"If it wasn't Veronica," I mused, "I'm not sure who it could be. I mean, I'm not running around like Sharon McCone, asking people questions. Otherwise I would consider it a warning from someone."

"The murderer?" Marylou's eyes grew round with horror.

"Most likely," I said, "but who might've got the wind up over what I've been doing?" I shook my head. "No, I think it's more likely just a malicious prank."

"If that rock had hit your head, or if you had hit your head hard on something when you fell, it could be a lot more serious," Marylou said.

"True," I responded as I began to grapple with the

implications of what Marylou had just said. Oddly enough, I hadn't really thought about the potential seriousness of what had happened to me. What if the rock thrower had intended something more vicious?

"No," I said, "if whoever threw the rock wanted to hurt me badly, she—or he—would have finished the job once I fell and passed out."

"Even so," Marylou said, her face taking on a stubborn cast, "your injury could be far worse. But, thank the Lord, it wasn't." She reached over and patted my knee.

"Amen to that," I said, and I meant it.

"What are you going to do about it?"

"What *can* I do about it?" I countered. "I've been thinking about it. I'll probably mention it to Deputy Ainsworth when I see him, but what can he do about it? I suppose he could ask some questions, try to find possible witnesses, but frankly I don't think there's much chance of proving who actually did it."

"That's frustrating," Marylou said. "I'd really like to find whoever did it and bash *them* over the head with a rock."

I had to laugh at that. The thought of gentle, motherly Marylou striking anyone with a rock was funny, to say the least.

"Who are you going to hit over the head?" Sophie asked as she walked into the room. As usual, she looked like she had just stepped from the pages of a fashion magazine.

"The person who hurt Emma," Marylou said.

"Good," Sophie replied with an evil grin. "I'll help you."

"My guardian angels," I said, looking from one to the other. Truth be told, I was touched by their obvious concern for me. If I hadn't had them with me, I probably would have been far more disturbed by the incident.

"I still say Emma should tell someone about this," Marylou insisted. "It ought to be reported."

"I know," I said gently, "and I promise you I will talk to Deputy Ainsworth about it when I get a chance."

"I think we should just go downstairs and get hold of Veronica," Sophie said. She stood in front of Marylou and me, her arms crossed over her chest. "Marylou and I will hold her, Emma, and you can punch her."

"Oh, right," I said. "I can just see me taking a swing at her." I shook my head, smiling. "No thank you."

"It was just a thought," Sophie replied, once again offering me that evil grin. "I tell you what—you and Marylou hold her, and *I'll* give her a punch or two."

"Goodness, you and Marylou are in a bloodthirsty mood this morning," I said, mock-severely.

"One for all, and all for one," Sophie said. Marylou chimed in with a vigorous "Amen."

I got up from the couch and set my coffee cup on a nearby table. "Well, my dear musketeers, how about some breakfast? If you're going to punch someone out, you're going to need something to give you the energy."

Laughing, we retrieved our handbags before we headed out the door.

Breakfast was a merry affair. The three of us carried on like high school girls, and it was a wonder someone didn't come to tell us to hold it down.

The waitress cleared our table and came back with the coffeepot. "Anything more, ladies?" She smiled at us, so evidently we hadn't been too out of control.

"Not for me, thanks," I said. After three cups, I had hit my limit—at least for now.

Sophie and Marylou also declined. Our waitress smiled again and walked over to another table.

"Time for some bridge, don't you think?" Marylou beamed.

"Of course," Sophie said.

"Let's go." I got up from my chair and picked up my bag.

As we left the dining room and approached the lobby, I spotted Veronica Hinkelmeier at the front desk. No one else was around. I was struck by an idea as we came nearer the desk.

Veronica hadn't spotted us yet. I halted and grabbed at Marylou and Sophie.

"What is it?" Sophie asked, puzzled.

"I've got an idea," I said in an undertone. "Just play along." They both nodded.

I resumed progress toward the front desk. "Good morning," I said when the three of us reached it.

Veronica turned slowly from the computer she had been using. "Good morning." The fake smile of welcome on her face disappeared for a moment; then with an obvious effort, she forced it back. "Is there something I can do for you, ladies?"

"Actually, there is," I said, keeping my tone pleasant. "I need a basket." I stopped and stared at her expectantly.

"A basket?" Veronica asked, plainly taken aback.

"Yes, a basket, about this big," I said, sketching the size in the air with my hands.

"We might have something like that," Veronica said, frowning. She was taking few pains to hide her irritation. "I'll have to check."

"Thank you," I said. Then, leaning forward in a

confiding manner, I continued. "You see, I need something like that to carry a rock in."

Veronica stiffened for a split second, and if I hadn't
been watching her carefully, I wouldn't have seen it.
"A rock?" She smiled. "That's rather unusual."

"Oh, yes," I said, "and this is an unusual rock. I
found it yesterday afternoon while I was out walking
on the trail through the woods." I paused a moment
for effect. "You might say it just hit me. That I had
to have it, I mean." I smiled sweetly at her.

Once again her body went completely still; then she
moved closer to the counter. "I'm not sure if we can
allow you to remove anything from the premises."

"Really?" Sophie asked. "That's a shame, because
we wanted to show this rock to one of the deputies."

Veronica didn't respond to that little gambit. She
simply stared balefully at Sophie.

"It's a very interesting rock," Sophie assured her,
"and I'm sure Emma wouldn't mind paying for it, if
you like."

"Naturally, I'd be willing to pay for it," I said. "But
of course, if I'm just going to show it to one of the
deputies, I suppose I don't really have to pay for it."

"Why would you want to waste their time showing
them a stupid rock?" The scorn in Veronica's voice
would probably have convinced someone else, but the
longer this conversation continued, the more sure I
was that Veronica was the rock thrower.

"Because we think they should test it for fingerprints," Marylou said. "You know, it's really amazing
these days, how they can get fingerprints from all
kinds of surfaces. And it sure would be interesting to
see whose fingerprints they can get off that rock."

The three of us stood there beaming at her, and she
didn't move for a long moment, her gaze fixed on the

counter between us. I noticed a vein throbbing in her forehead, and her breath was just a bit labored.

She raised her eyes to meet mine, and I glimpsed the guilt there. Then she tossed her head and turned away, facing her computer again.

"I don't have time for this stupidity," she said. "I have work to do."

Sophie stepped closer and rapped on the counter. "Look at me, Veronica," she said, her tone fierce.

Startled, Veronica turned back toward the counter.

"We know what you did, and you're just lucky Emma wasn't badly hurt," Sophie said in a calmer voice. "If you try anything like that again, I'll personally beat the crap out of you."

"And I'll help," Marylou said.

I merely smiled.

Veronica said something terribly rude and disappeared through the door behind the counter. She didn't quite slam it, but it certainly closed firmly.

"That settles that, I guess," Marylou said.

"I think we ought to talk to the owners about her," Sophie said. "She needs to be fired, and right away."

"No, let it go," I said. "We really can't prove anything, because I don't think they really can get fingerprints from rock. I'll talk to Ainsworth about it at some point, like I said, and leave it up to him."

"You're probably right, but I want her to be punished." Sophie said.

"Look at it this way," Marylou said with a smile. "She has to look at herself in the mirror every day. That's punishment enough." She had raised her voice, and I wondered if Veronica heard her.

"Bridge," I said in a firm tone. "Let's play bridge." I headed for the ballroom.

"Before we do that," Marylou said, huffing a little

as she caught up with me, "why don't we go look at the exhibits? There are people here with all kinds of things for sale, and we might find something fun."

"Fine with me," Sophie said.

"I really ought to get some kind of souvenir for Jack and Luke," I said, thinking of my brother and his partner. They were as bridge-mad as Marylou. "Where are the exhibits?"

"Down the hall from the ballroom, I think," Sophie said.

We passed the ballroom, already a hive of activity. Farther down the hall there was another large space, and this was, as Sophie said, where the exhibitors were displaying and selling their wares.

Pausing at the threshold, we took a moment to survey the room. There were probably twenty-five or thirty booths, and a number of people were milling about, chatting with exhibitors and examining various items on display.

I spotted a booth with a lot of books, and I headed for that one first. Marylou and Sophie wandered off in the other direction.

"Good morning." An attractive young man smiled at me as I approached the books. His name tag read DAVID.

I returned his greeting.

"Let me know if I can help you with anything," he said.

"Thank you," I responded. "I will."

I could never resist the lure of books, and I spent a happy fifteen minutes or so examining bridge books of all kinds. Books to help me with my bidding, books on defense, books on conventions—book after book on how to play bridge. I found a slim volume on the history of the game, and I perused it a bit more thoroughly.

I had never really read much about the history of bridge, and this book looked like a good resource. It also had a section on the history of playing cards, and after skimming it briefly, I decided I definitely wanted to purchase it.

Then something in this section caught my eye, and I felt a slight tingle of excitement.

Had I just stumbled on a possibly important clue to the identity of the killer?

Chapter 21

After I paid for the books I had chosen, the young man bundled them into a bag with a handle. He thanked me for my purchase, and I smiled back at him.

My thoughts centered on what I had read about the history of playing cards. I needed time, however, to sit down and read the book slowly and carefully. I might be wildly off base, but if I wasn't, then I might have found a very important clue.

"Emma!"

Marylou's voice snapped me out of my brief reverie. She was beckoning from a few booths away, and I walked over to her. Should I say anything to her and Sophie about what I had discovered?

No, I decided. *Not just yet.*

"What have you found?" I asked.

"Aren't these adorable?" Marylou pointed to sets of earrings made in the shapes of the four card suits.

I picked up a pair of spade earrings and examined them closely. The workmanship was actually quite good. The spades themselves were made of onyx, and not merely black enamel as I had first thought. The setting was gold, forming a thin border around each spade.

The other suits were equally well crafted. The clubs were also onyx, and the diamonds and hearts were a deep red.

"Red jasper," the woman at the booth replied in answer to my query.

"They're exquisitely made," I said, and she thanked me.

They were also expensive, I noted, and I eyed the diamonds with regret. I could afford them, but I always hesitated to spend that much money on clothes or jewelry.

"Go ahead and buy them." Sophie spoke from behind me, startling me. "You know you want them."

"Yes, do, Emma," Marylou said. "They're lovely."

Well, how could I not buy them after that? Sophie would nag me if I didn't, or Marylou would probably buy them for me for my next birthday. I knew my two friends all too well.

"I'm going to buy a couple of pairs myself," Marylou said. "I want a pair of spades and one of hearts."

"I'll take clubs," Sophie said, grinning at me.

"And I'll have the diamonds," I said, not too reluctantly, truth be told.

Then I spotted something else. "And I'll take two sets of cuff links," I said, thinking of Jack and Luke. Their anniversary was coming up in a couple of months, and these cuff links would be a perfect gift. They had met in college over a bridge table and had been together ever since. "One set of spades and one of hearts." I handed over my credit card, determined not to wince at the amount.

"Good idea," Sophie said. "They'll love them."

Our purchases paid for and neatly boxed, we continued on our survey of the room. We viewed a wide array of products, more jewelry, more books, all kinds of cards and scorepads, computer software, and more. There was even a booth for a travel agent whose specialty was bridge vacations. We had to tear Marylou away from that one, but she brought away with her a handful of brochures.

"Don't you think a cruise sounds heavenly?" she said, beaming at Sophie and me.

"They're very relaxing," Sophie said.

"I've never been on one," I said. "Baxter and I always talked about it, but we never got around to taking one." For a moment I thought I would burst into tears. The grief hit me suddenly.

Sophie squeezed my arm, and I held on to my self-control. "Sorry," I said, trying to swallow the lump in my throat.

"Don't apologize," Marylou said, in a soft voice. "We understand." She slipped an arm around me and gave me a quick hug.

"Thank you," I said. Then, my voice stronger, I continued. "What say we go put these things away in our suite, then come back down and play some bridge?" I brandished my small bag of books and the jewelry. "I don't really want to tote these around with me."

"An excellent idea," Sophie said. She led the way to the elevator.

Exiting the elevator on our floor, we walked past the scene of the crime. The closed door to Avery Trowbridge's suite still bore crime scene tape, and I shuddered slightly as we approached our suite.

Inside we each stowed our purchases, and as I was about to put away the bag of books, I paused. I remembered the book on the history of bridge and its section on playing cards. Perhaps I should sit down right now and study it instead of going downstairs to play bridge with the others. They probably wouldn't think it too strange if I decided to stay here in the suite because of what had happened yesterday.

I could tell them why I wanted to stay in the suite and read this particular book, but what if I was way off base in what I was thinking? I doubted they would laugh at me for my flight of fancy. They weren't like that. Still, I felt reluctance over sharing my ideas with them until I had more time to read and ponder. Then I could use them as a sounding board before approaching Deputy Ainsworth.

"Ready?" Sophie asked, coming out of the bathroom after touching up her makeup.

"I've changed my mind," I said, sitting down on my bed. "Would you and Marylou mind terribly if I stayed here in the room? I think I'll relax and read for a while."

Sophie's eyes grew big with concern. "Are you okay? Do you have a headache? Nausea?"

I laughed. "No, nothing like that. I just thought I'd like a little quiet time."

"Okay," Sophie said. "You know best, and the doctor said you shouldn't overdo it, anyway." She came over to me and gave me a quick hug. "Are you sure you wouldn't like one of us to stay here with you, just in case?"

"No," I said in a firm tone. "I'll be fine. You two go on and play, and I'll join you for lunch. Around one?"

"See you then," Sophie said, moving toward the door but casting glances over her shoulder at me.

"Go!" I pointed to the door. "And tell Marylou not to fuss."

"Yes, ma'am," she said, grinning.

Moments later I heard Marylou exclaiming as Sophie told her I wanted to stay in the room. Despite Sophie's best efforts, Marylou shrugged her off and came into the bedroom. "Honey, are you sure everything's okay?"

Touched though I was by her concern, I was beginning to feel a bit exasperated. "I'm fine," I said. "I just want to relax awhile. Go play bridge." I smiled to take any sting out of my words.

"If you're sure," Marylou said, still sounding doubtful.

"I'm sure." I made shooing motions with my hands.

"See you at lunch," Marylou said, shaking her head as she left the room.

Seconds later, the outer door closed behind them, and I breathed a sigh of relief. I loved them both dearly, but I also enjoyed time on my own sometimes. This was one of those times.

I picked up the bridge-history book and carried it with me into the living room. Making myself comfortable in one corner of the sofa, I switched on the lamp next to me and began to read.

The first section of the book dealt with the origin of playing cards as we know them today. Some scholars, I read, believed that cards originated in China after the invention of paper there. A few others suggested that they might have come from India, but there appeared to be little research to back that up, at least in this book.

There was dispute over when and how playing cards were introduced to Europe. Some thought it was the Mamelukes of Egypt who had brought them in the late fourteenth century. I paused for a moment, trying to remember who or what the Mamelukes were. Then

I noticed a footnote. This explained that they were basically slave soldiers who converted to Islam and served some of the Islamic leaders during the Middle Ages. They sometimes seized power for themselves, however, and this they had done in Egypt in the mid-thirteenth century, remaining in power for over 250 years.

Now that I had a better sense of who the Mamelukes were, I continued reading the main text. In the late fourteenth and early fifteenth centuries, the use of playing cards spread widely across Europe. Apparently most of the cards of the time, at least surviving examples of them, were made from woodcuts printed on paper. From this point on, Europeans experimented with the design of the cards, and by the end of the fifteenth century, the four suits now almost universally used originated in France.

Then I reached the bit that had caught my eye earlier. In France around this time, there were two basic designs for the cards, one from Rouen and the other, Paris. In the Rouen system, the kings of spades, hearts, diamonds, and clubs represented, respectively, David, Alexander, Caesar, and Charlemagne. The queens were said to be Pallas, the Greek warrior goddess; Rachel, the biblical mother of Joseph; Argine, the origin of which name was obscure, though possibly an anagram of *regina,* the Latin word for "queen"; and, finally, Judith, the biblical heroine who slew the invader Holofernes.

In Parisian tradition, the same names were used, but assigned to different suits. The kings, in suit order, were David, Charlemagne (or Charles), Caesar, and Alexander, while the queens were Pallas, Judith, Rachel, and Argine. There were also different names assigned to the jacks, or knaves, but at the moment I didn't think they were particularly significant. I was more interested in the queens and whom they represented.

When I found Avery Trowbridge dead, he was clutching the queen of diamonds in his hand.

Was that a mere coincidence? Or had he grasped the card from the table as a signal to the identity of his killer?

A man who made his living teaching and playing bridge would certainly understand the significance of a particular card.

I looked at the list of queens again. In the Rouen set, the queen of diamonds represented the mysterious Argine. That seemed too obscure to me to be of real use.

In the Parisian tradition, however, the queen of diamonds represented Rachel, the biblical mother of Joseph. Did that mean Lorraine Trowbridge, the mother of Avery's son?

Then it hit me. Rachel was the *second* wife of Jacob. He had married Rachel's sister Leah first.

Was Avery Trowbridge trying to tell everyone that his murderer was his second wife, Paula?

Chapter 22

I put the book aside and tried to think this through as clearly as possible.

First, did the card in Avery Trowbridge's hand really mean anything?

To answer that, I forced myself to remember what I had seen, the position of the body and the cards on the table. Was it likely that Avery had been holding any cards in his hands when he confronted his killer? He would have seen the killer, even if someone had tried to sneak up on him. His chair was in the corner, its back too near the wall for someone to slip behind it without being seen.

The killer was probably someone Avery didn't consider a serious threat. He might have been fiddling with the cards on the board and not been paying much attention to the killer. The killer caught him unawares, and Avery, clutching the queen of diamonds, died in the chair.

That was a possibility, particularly if Avery died instantly from the blow. Then I remembered the blood. There was too much of it for Avery to have died instantly. His heart continued to pump blood for at least a few seconds after the knife entered his chest.

He therefore might have had just enough strength to reach to the table and pick up a card. Then he collapsed in the chair and died.

What about the killer, though? Wouldn't the killer have stood by and waited until he or she was sure Avery was dead?

Possibly, I decided, in which case my theory about the card could be all wrong.

Unless, that is, the killer put that specific card in Avery's hand. That bore some thought.

If the killer had immediately fled the scene, though, horrified by what she had just done, she might not have seen Avery's last, desperate act.

That was possible, too.

Back to the idea that the killer had placed the card in Avery's hand—who hated Paula so much that he wanted to point the finger at her?

I doubted that Lorraine Trowbridge or Veronica Hinkelmeier had any love for Paula. And Basil Dumont might have done it out of spite. Kill Avery to rid himself of a detested professional rival, and at the same time perhaps put his ex-wife behind bars for murder. I wasn't so certain, despite Paula's blithe assurance, that Basil really wanted her back.

So the card in Avery's hand could be an attempt to frame Paula—if I was interpreting the card and its significance correctly, that Rachel equaled Paula and not Lorraine.

What if it *was* meant to identify Lorraine?

Rachel was the mother of Joseph, Jacob's eleventh and best-loved son. Since Avery had only the one son—at least only one that I knew about—Rachel could possibly equal Lorraine in this case.

I kept coming back to the fact, however, that Rachel

was Jacob's *second* wife, and that had to indicate Paula, not Lorraine.

Unless Avery had been married to someone else before he was married to Lorraine.

The more I considered that solution, the more I liked it. I really hated to think of Marylou's friend Paula as a killer. It was easier for me to cast Lorraine in that role because I barely knew her.

How could I find out whether Avery had been married three times?

I could ask either Lorraine or Paula, and they would both no doubt think I was being incredibly nosy, if not ghoulish.

Or, I thought, feeling pleased with myself, I could ask Haskell Crenshaw, Avery's business manager. He might very well know, and I wouldn't mind asking him a few other questions besides. He was still a contender for the role of killer, despite the clue of the diamond queen, as I thought of it semihumorously. That sounded like the title of a Nancy Drew book.

Stop it, I told myself. *Focus, and stop being silly.*

What about Veronica? I wondered. Could the queen of diamonds somehow refer to her?

Not as Rachel, I decided, but what about as Argine? The book had little to say about the identity of Argine. The significance of that name was probably lost. Maybe it was more likely that it was an anagram of *regina.* Could Veronica be considered a queen?

Queen of the bitches, I thought in a moment of sheer cattiness. Seriously, though, I doubted it referred to Veronica.

But what about Haskell Crenshaw? The term "queen" could be used, sometimes spitefully, to refer to a gay man.

If that was the case, though, why the queen of diamonds?

Maybe it was the first queen Avery saw in his attempt to leave a clue to his killer's identity.

That might mean that the true significance of the card was that it was a queen, and any of the four queens would have sufficed. Avery just happened to pick up the queen of diamonds.

Pleased with this bit of reasoning, I mulled it over. Crenshaw certainly had a motive for killing Avery. That knife in the chest could be construed as an act of passion. If Avery had humiliated him both professionally *and* personally, it might have been more than Crenshaw could bear. Men had been driven to murder for less.

If, if, if. All I had were theories, no real, hard facts. If the card meant something, it could be any of several possibilities. Was I simply wasting my time in silly speculation?

So much for being Nancy Drew. I decided it was time for action. I might as well be downstairs playing bridge. I glanced at the clock. Only a little over an hour now before I was supposed to meet Marylou and Sophie for lunch.

I used the bathroom, then checked myself in the mirror. The bare minimum of makeup that I wore didn't need much retouching. I was on my way downstairs moments later.

In the elevator I considered whether I should go to Deputy Ainsworth and tell him my ideas about the significance of the queen of diamonds. At first I had been really excited by the possibility that I had found an important clue to the killer's identity. The more I mulled it over, however, the more uncertain I was that it actually meant anything. Ainsworth might think I was a complete idiot for even wasting his time on something like this.

On the other hand . . . *Oh, stop it!* I admonished myself as the elevator doors slid open on the first floor. *Stop being so wishy-washy.* When I next saw the deputy, I would tell him what I thought the card could mean, and he could take it from there. And if he thought I was a complete nutcase, then he would just have to think it.

I stepped off the elevator and took a few steps in the direction of the ballroom, then halted.

Maybe I should try to find the deputy and talk to him right away. Yes, best to get it over with, I decided.

I turned in the other direction and headed for the corridor where the sheriff's department had set up its headquarters for the investigation.

Pausing on the threshold of the room, I glanced around, hoping to see Deputy Ainsworth. He didn't appear to be there, and I didn't know whether to be irritated or relieved.

"Can I help you, ma'am?"

The person addressing me was the young female deputy who had accompanied Ainsworth yesterday. I glanced discreetly at her name tag. "Um, Deputy Jordan, I was hoping to find Deputy Ainsworth."

"He's not here right now, Mrs. Diamond," she said. "Is there something I can help you with?"

I hesitated for a moment. I could explain everything to her; then she could convey it all to her superior. If he wanted to question me further, he could. If he didn't, well, I wouldn't have to worry about it anymore.

"Yes, there is," I said after a pause that went on just a bit too long.

"Why don't you come over here and sit down?"

Deputy Jordan conducted me to a desk on the other side of the room. She indicated a chair by the desk, and I sat down.

"It's about the card that Avery Trowbridge had in his hand," I said. I waited a moment, and she nodded encouragement.

"I found a book on the history of bridge," I said, "and one section of the book tells about the history of playing cards." I could see her trying to hide her impatience. I hurried on. "The different face cards originally were symbols for historic persons, and it's just possible that Avery Trowbridge was trying to tell us something by holding the queen of diamonds."

"Like what?" Suddenly, Deputy Jordan appeared more interested in what I had to say.

"Bear with me," I said. "This will take a few minutes." As succinctly as I could, I explained the symbolism of the cards, and then I told her my theories about the queen of diamonds. At some point I realized she had begun jotting notes on a pad of paper.

"Go on," she said when I paused.

"That's about it," I said. "It all may not mean a blessed thing, but I thought you should know, just in case."

"So you don't think the card refers to you?" A suspicion of smile lurked around her lips.

"No, I don't," I said tartly. "I had only met the man the day before, and I had no reason to kill him. My name is just a coincidence in this case."

"Yes, ma'am," Deputy Jordan said, smiling broadly now. She stood up. "Thank you for telling me about this, Mrs. Diamond. I'll make sure Deputy Ainsworth hears about this. He may have more questions for you."

"Of course," I said, standing up also. "I'm sure he'll

be able to find me if he wants to talk to me. Thank you, Deputy." I turned away and walked toward the door. Once there, I paused and looked back. Jordan was on her cell phone, talking to someone. I hoped it was Ainsworth.

Out in the corridor, I glanced at my watch. It was about ten minutes till I was supposed to meet Sophie and Marylou in the dining room. I might as well wait there.

I stopped in the doorway of the dining room and looked around to see whether my dining companions had arrived early.

They hadn't, and I was about to turn back and have a seat in the waiting area when I spotted someone waving at me from a table near one of the windows.

I waved back, and Will Trowbridge indicated that he wanted me to join him. *Why not?* I thought. I doubted that Marylou and Sophie would mind, and when Sophie joined us, I was sure she would charm Will to no end. She generally had that effect on men of any age.

"Hello, Will," I said as I reached the table.

He stood up. "Hello, Mrs. Diamond. Please sit with me. I really hate to eat alone."

He held my chair for me, and I sat down, feeling about a hundred years old. I wasn't used to such courtly gestures from young men. "Thank you." He ducked his head, looking slightly embarrassed.

Resuming his seat, Will said, "I haven't ordered yet, but the waitress ought to be back in a minute with my tea." He opened his mouth to say something else, but no words came out. He fixed his gaze on the tablecloth.

I smiled. He really did seem to be a nice boy, and I felt sorry for him, being no doubt dragged here by his mother. Before I could say anything, the waitress appeared with Will's tea. "I'll have the same," I told her. She nodded and walked away.

"Is your mother playing bridge this morning?" I asked.

Will nodded. "She's as nutty about bridge as my dad was." A spasm of pain crossed his face. "God, I hate this." His clenched hands rested on the table in front of him.

"I know," I reached over to pat one of his hands. "It's way beyond awful, and I wish there were more I could do to help you, Will."

"I'm okay," he said, looking anything but okay. "I've just got to get used to it."

I didn't want to tell him that I didn't think you could ever completely "get used to it," because that wasn't what he needed to hear right now. Instead I said, "You should concentrate on the good memories as much as possible, and let everything else go. I know it's hard, but if you can do that, it does help."

He nodded.

To try distracting him, I asked him about college. He was studying history, I discovered, and he was passionately interested in Elizabethan England. We stopped our discussion long enough to order our meals, and when the food came, we both ate without tasting much of it, I realized later. He was very knowledgeable, as well as very articulate. He was the kind of student I always dreamed of having and encountered only once in a blue moon.

Suddenly Will broke off as he glanced over my shoulder. "Oh, great," he said, "speak of the devil."

"What do you mean?" I asked, startled.

"Here comes Her Majesty," he said, sarcasm dripping from the words. "Lorraine Regina herself." He pronounced "Regina" in the British fashion, "re-JI-nuh."

My eyes widened in surprise. "Why do you call her that?"

"That's what Dad always called her," Will said, leaning forward and whispering. She must have been getting close to us. "Regina is her middle name, and that's Latin for 'queen.'"

Chapter 23

"Are you okay?" Will asked me.

I nodded. "I'm fine."

"You sure look funny," he said, seeming not entirely convinced.

"No, really," I said, "I'm okay." I smiled to reassure him, though actually I felt anything but okay. My mind was racing with the implications of what I had just learned. Suddenly, my food wasn't sitting too well in my stomach.

"Will, I thought you were going to lunch with me," Lorraine Trowbridge said, sliding into an empty chair between her son and me. She gave me a cool glance.

Will reddened. "You're almost an hour later than you said you'd be."

"I see you found someone else to share your meal," Lorraine said, deigning to smile at me.

"Yes, Will was kind enough to invite me to share his table," I said. I kept my voice cool. "I dislike eating alone, and I'm sure Will does, too. We had quite an interesting chat, actually."

"Really?" Lorraine said, one eyebrow raised. "And what did you two find to chatter about?"

"History," Will said, almost spitting out the word. "Something that doesn't interest you."

Lorraine laughed. "You really shouldn't bore other people with this obsession of yours, Will."

I wanted to slap the woman. I couldn't bear seeing the hurt in her son's eyes. "On the contrary, Lorraine, I found Will anything *but* boring. I'm *obsessed* with history as much as he is. In fact, I used to teach it." I paused for a moment to let that sink in. "I think your son will make a first-rate historian, and if there's ever anything I can do to help him"—here I turned to face Will—"then I will be delighted to do so."

Will acknowledged my words by nodding slightly; then he ducked his head in embarrassment. Lorraine appeared not in the least fazed by my little speech. She shrugged.

"I'm glad he found such a kindred spirit," she said. She raised a hand to summon a waitress. "I'm sure you'll excuse us, Emma, but I'd like to talk to my son in private."

By now I shouldn't have been surprised by the woman's rudeness, but I was still taken aback. "Certainly," I said, trying to hold on to my temper. I thought briefly about dashing the contents of my water glass in her face, but that would be childish.

Instead, I rose from my seat and picked up my bag. "Will, thank you for a delightful conversation. I enjoyed every minute of it." I let my gaze rest upon Lorraine, and she stared back at me. I molded my face into an expression that I had seen my mother use more times than I could count. I called it her "I just saw a nasty bug" face. I held it for a few seconds. Then I smiled.

Lorraine blinked and the color rose quickly in her face. She opened her mouth, but nothing came out.

"Have a nice day," I said, turned, and walked away. Behind me I heard what sounded like smothered laughter.

I probably should have been ashamed of myself for behaving like that, but I actually enjoyed it. Lorraine Trowbridge was a nasty woman, and I wasn't going to waste any remorse over her. I did feel awfully sorry for her son, though.

Lorraine *Regina* Trowbridge, I remembered. Because of the woman's shoddy behavior, I had briefly forgotten what Will told me.

Regina. An anagram of "Argine." The queen of diamonds in the Rouen tradition of naming the face cards.

Maybe Avery was trying to tell us that Lorraine was the killer. He even called her that, according to what Will had said. Other people might be aware of the nickname, too, so Avery could count on someone informing the authorities.

I was so lost in thought that I wasn't paying attention to where I was going. Suddenly, I felt hands on my arms, and someone said, "Hang on, Emma."

I stopped and focused. "Sophie, Marylou," I said. "I'm sorry, I forgot all about you."

"We know," Sophie said with a laugh.

"We saw you in the dining room with Will Trowbridge," Marylou said, "and you seemed so wrapped up in your conversation we decided not to interrupt."

"What on earth were you two talking about so intensely?" Sophie asked.

As we talked, Sophie and Marylou led me in the direction of the ballroom.

"History," I said. "Will told me that he's a history major, and his favorite period is Elizabethan England. That's what we were talking about."

"I might have known," Sophie said, shaking her head. "No wonder you didn't see us."

I laughed. "No, sorry."

"What do you think of Will?" Marylou asked. We had reached the ballroom, and we stood to one side of the doors, still in the corridor.

"He's a very nice young man with a nasty shrew for a mother," I said, and I told them how Lorraine had behaved when she joined us at the table.

"What a cow," Sophie said. "I would call her something worse, but Marylou would have a fit." She grinned.

Marylou laughed. "I don't know—in this case I might let you get away with it. How could she treat her own son that way?" She shook her head. "That poor boy."

"So you don't think he's the killer?" Sophie dropped her voice to a whisper as several people walked past us into the ballroom.

"No, I don't think so," I said. "Look, I've got a lot to tell you. Can we skip playing bridge for a little while? We need to talk, and we ought to do it in private."

"Of course," Marylou said. "Let's go upstairs."

Sophie led the way to the elevator, and we were soon on our way upstairs. "Can't you give us a hint?" Sophie asked as we stepped out onto our floor.

I looked around, and since there didn't seem to be anyone about, I said, "I found what I think might be a really important clue to the killer's identity."

Sophie's eyes widened, and Marylou inhaled sharply.

"We certainly don't want to talk about it out here in the hall," Marylou said, putting on speed. "Come on, I can't wait to hear this."

I had never seen Marylou move quite so fast, and Sophie and I hustled to catch up to her.

We were all a little breathless by the time we reached our suite. Marylou fumbled with the key, and Sophie had to take over so we could get into the room.

"Sorry," Marylou said, laughing a little. "I guess I'm too excited."

Sophie shut the door behind us and then pointed to the sofa. "Sit down, and start talking."

I made myself comfortable on the sofa, while Marylou sat down at the other end. Sophie pulled a chair close and plopped down in it.

"Okay," I said, "this will take a little while, so just bear with me."

Once again, I launched into my story about the clue of the diamond queen. I gave them the long version of the history of playing cards, and they didn't interrupt me or look skeptical the way Deputy Jordan had earlier.

I wasn't sure how long I talked, but by the time I finished, my throat was dry. "I need some water," I said, starting to get up. I shifted on the sofa, putting my hands down on the cushions as I did so. My left hand slipped into the gap between the cushion and the arm of the sofa, and it encountered something slick and stiff.

"Don't get up," Sophie said, jumping up from her chair. "I'll get you some water."

"Thanks," I said. My fingers closed around the object. It was thin and pliable, and I realized what it was before I pulled it loose from its resting place.

It was a playing card. I stared at the familiar design on the back of it, a card from a Bicycle deck. I turned it over. It was the king of spades.

What on earth was it doing in our sofa?

Chapter 24

A knock sounded on our door, and almost without thought, I shoved the king of spades back into its hiding place in the sofa.

Marylou had seen the card in my hand and started to ask me about it, but I shook my head.

The knocking started again, and this time a voice called out, "Yoo-hoo! Anyone in there?"

It was Paula Trowbridge, and Marylou got up from the sofa to answer the door.

Sophie came back with a glass of water for me, and I smiled my thanks before taking a sip. In the meantime my mind was busy trying to decide whether the presence of that card in the sofa had any significance. I needed to examine it more closely, but that would have to wait.

"I'm so glad you're all here," Paula said, practically bounding into the room. "I have such wonderful news." Her eyes sparkled, and her cheeks flushed becomingly.

"Have a seat, dear, and tell us all about it," Marylou said, guiding Paula to the spot she had just occupied on the sofa.

Paula sat, but she was so excited she bounced a

little. Marylou found a chair and brought it close, while Sophie resumed her seat. I sipped at my water and eyed Paula with great interest.

"Oh, it's just the most wonderful news," Paula said. In my brief acquaintance with her I had never seen her in an ebullient mood like this.

"You already said that," Sophie told her in a slightly damping tone.

Paula didn't notice. "It's Basil," she said. She looked from one to the other of us, swiveling her head slightly in order to include Marylou.

"What about Basil?" Marylou asked.

"It's just so thrilling," Paula said. If her voice went any higher, every dog in the area would soon converge on our suite.

"Calm down," Marylou said, her voice stern. "You're just babbling. Settle down, and tell us what this is all about."

Paula grimaced, but she made a visible effort to comply with Marylou's commands. "Basil wants me to marry him." Again, she looked at each of us in turn, no doubt expecting hearty congratulations or other expressions of joy.

"I'm sure that makes you very happy," Marylou said, and Sophie and I chimed in with our congratulations.

"Thank you," Paula said, and if she noticed our less-than-enthusiastic reception of her news, she didn't give any signs. "But there's more." She paused, simpering at each of us in turn.

"Yes," I said, "what else?" If one of us didn't play along, we might be sitting here for hours. Honestly, she was like a child with a big secret to tell.

"Basil's been offered the most wonderful deal," Paula said, squirming ecstatically. "He's going to take over a nationally syndicated bridge column. The man who's been doing it for forever had to stop doing it for health reasons, and they called Basil today to ask him if he would do it. And he said yes."

"I'm sure that's very exciting for him," Sophie said.

"Please be sure to offer him our congratulations," Marylou said.

"Oh, you can tell him yourself," Paula said, giggling. "He should be here any minute, along with the champagne."

"Champagne?" I asked. "Is he bringing champagne?"

"No, silly," Paula said, "the hotel is sending some up. I asked them to, because I thought we could have a little party. I wanted to celebrate, and where better to do it than with my friends?"

I was more than a little taken aback by Paula's assumption that we would be happy to host a party in our suite for a man we really didn't know. Marylou and Sophie were just as surprised as I was. I also thought it was more than a bit strange to be celebrating Basil Dumont's triumph in the suite next to a crime scene. The man's rival had been murdered just feet away from where we were all sitting. Apparently that hadn't occurred to Paula, or if it had, it certainly hadn't bothered her.

"Paula, dear," Marylou said, "I'm not sure we're equipped for a party."

"It's just champagne," Paula said, waving a hand in the air. "No food or anything. Basil and I just wanted to be able to celebrate a little. After all, we couldn't really do it in public, now, could we? That would be tacky, and what would people think?"

"Yes, indeed, what *would* people think?" Sophie said.

Someone knocked at the door, and this time Sophie

answered it. She admitted Basil Dumont, and before she could close the door, a room service waiter appeared with an iced bottle of champagne and glasses.

The waiter wheeled the cart bearing the champagne into the room, and Basil signed for it with a flourish. As the waiter left the room, Basil turned to us with a smile. "Good afternoon, ladies. Thank you for joining in my little celebration."

Marylou, Sophie, and I exchanged glances. They were as disconcerted as I was by this turn of events. But what could we do? We couldn't just throw them out of our suite.

Instead, we greeted him, and he turned his attention to the champagne. Moments later the cork popped, and Basil filled the glasses and handed us each one. Paula jumped up from the couch, almost spilling her champagne, and joined Basil standing before us.

Basil raised his glass and said, "Here's to my own bridge column. I've wanted this for a very long time, and now I've got it. It's really a dream come true." He sipped from his glass.

Marylou, Sophie, and I murmured words of congratulations, but he was so wrapped up in self-satisfaction that he really paid little attention to us. Paula stared at him with adoring eyes, and she bolted back most of her champagne before seizing him around the neck and giving him a vigorous hug.

Basil disentangled himself from his former wife—none too gently in my opinion—and refilled his glass. "This really is a fantastic opportunity for me," he told us. "This means my name will be in thousands of newspapers all across the country. And the more my name is out there, the more opportunities I'll have. I'll finally be on the A-list for cruises, and it should help me internationally as well." He drank from his glass.

"That's wonderful for you," Marylou said. Sophie and I nodded.

Paula had wilted a bit, and her lower lip trembled. "Basil, darling, that's not *all* the good news."

"Hmm? What do you mean?" Puzzled, he stared at her. Then realization hit him. "Oh, of course, how silly of me." He turned to face Marylou, Sophie, and me. "Paula and I are to be married again."

He said the words with an obvious effort at enthusiasm, but I didn't think he was very convincing. Sophie and I exchanged glances. Paula, however, seemed oblivious as usual. She brightened visibly once Basil had spoken.

"Isn't it wonderful?" Paula said. "I'm so happy. Basil and I really belong together, you know."

"Congratulations," Marylou said, and Sophie and I added our words of felicitation.

Paula was the only one excited, however, because Basil had turned morose. Whenever Paula wasn't looking at him, he had an odd expression on his face, like that of a trapped animal. Whenever she turned to look at him, however, he mustered up a semblance of happiness.

Conversation lagged. I had no idea what else to say to the supposedly happy couple, nor did Sophie. Even Marylou, who had known Paula a long time, couldn't seem to come up with anything to say. What had begun as bizarre became more and more painfully surreal.

Paula burbled on for a couple of minutes about all the things that she and Basil would be doing together, while Basil grew more and more fidgety. He took advantage of one of Paula's few pauses for breath and said, "Paula, I'm afraid I have to get back downstairs. I really should be on hand if anyone needs me." He set his empty glass on the cart beside the champagne bucket.

"Oh, sure," Paula said, frowning. "I forgot all about that. I guess I was just so excited, I forgot you're actually working." She put her glass alongside Basil's and turned to us. "Thank you so much for sharing this little celebration with us. It means so much to Basil and me to know our friends are happy for us."

Marylou got up from her chair and went to Paula, giving her a brief hug. "Of course we're happy for you, Paula," she said. "And we wish you both all the best."

"Yes, certainly," I said.

"Congratulations again," Sophie told them. She stood up, reached for my empty glass, and placed it along with hers on the cart.

"Thank you," Basil said. "Well, I must go." He gave Paula an awkward pat on the shoulder, and he almost bolted from the room.

Paula stared after him, and when the door closed behind him, she turned to us with a goofy look on her face. "He's so dedicated," she sighed. "Bridge is the most important thing in the world to him."

Did she not realize the significance of what she said? I wondered. If she didn't, she was completely delusional.

"I'm just glad that I'll be with him again, and I'll do whatever I can to boost his career," Paula said, smiling.

"Yes, I'm sure you'll do your best," Marylou said. She wheeled the cart to the door, opened it, and thrust the cart out into the hall.

She came back and took a firm hold of Paula's arm. "I know you'll excuse us, dear," she said as she steered her friend to the door, "but Emma, Sophie, and I need to freshen up before we go downstairs to play bridge again."

"Oh, of course," Paula said. "Well, thanks for celebrating with us." She opened the door and walked out into the hall. Marylou quickly closed the door behind her. "See you later," we heard Paula call.

"That was certainly strange," Marylou said. She resumed her place on the sofa, and Sophie sat down in her chair.

"Strange doesn't even *begin* to cover it," Sophie said. "How oblivious can she be?"

"Oh, I think deep down she knows," Marylou said. "She knows she comes second with Basil. Bridge is always first, but she's willing to accept that."

"I really do feel sorry for her," I said. "But it's her choice."

"I'm not sure it's Basil's," Sophie said. "Did you see the look on his face when she reminded him about their marriage?"

"That was a deer in the headlights if I ever saw one," I said. "He seems stuck with her."

"They probably deserve each other," Sophie said.

"Enough about them," Marylou said with a touch of impatience in her voice. "What I want to know, Emma, is, what was that you found just before Paula arrived?"

"Ah," I said, "yes. Hang on a minute." I got up from the sofa and went to the bathroom for a tissue. Back in the living room, tissue in hand, I extracted the king of spades from the corner of the sofa. "It was this." I held it up for Sophie and Marylou to see.

"A card?" Marylou said, frowning. "How strange."

"The king of spades," Sophie said. "And what is that in the corner?"

I turned the card so that the king faced me. I frowned. I hadn't noticed the spot before, but I hadn't had much time to examine it before Paula knocked on the door.

"It's reddish brown," I said. "Yuck. It looks like it might be blood." I laid the card down on the sofa beside me. The card was an important clue. I just wasn't sure of its significance yet.

"You don't think . . ." Marylou's voice trailed off.

I nodded. "I do think. I think this came from the deck Avery Trowbridge was using when he was murdered."

Chapter 25

"Then how did it get here, of all places?" Marylou asked me.

"I'll give you my guess," Sophie said. She and I exchanged looks. I knew we were thinking the same thing.

"How?" Marylou said.

"Who was sitting on that sofa yesterday morning, where Emma is sitting now?" Sophie watched as comprehension slowly dawned on Marylou's face.

"Paula," she said slowly.

"Exactly," I said.

"Were you with her the whole time?" Sophie asked. "I went into the bedroom for a little while, and you two were on the sofa when I left and when I came back."

"Yes," Marylou said, "I went to get her some aspirin out of my bag at one point, and I brought her a glass of water with the aspirin. So I was out of the room for a couple of minutes."

"More than time enough for her to hide the card in our sofa," I said.

"Yes, I can see that," Marylou said. "But why are you so convinced it was Paula? I mean, why couldn't it have been Veronica Hinkelmeier?"

I hadn't thought of that, and neither had Sophie. We stared at each other.

"We've been out of the room often enough, and long enough, for her to have sneaked in with a pass-key," Sophie said. "And we already know she has a grudge against Emma."

"It's certainly a possibility," I said, "but if she really did do it, why hasn't she thought up some reason for the sheriff's department to search and find it by now? I'd think she wouldn't want to wait very long to do that without delay."

"Who does the king of spades represent?" Sophie asked. "Maybe it has something to do with that?"

I thought for a moment about the reading I had done. "You know, I'm not completely sure," I said. "It's either David or Charlemagne, but I can't remember which." I got up from the sofa. "Hang on a moment, and I'll look it up."

In the bedroom I found the book and opened it to the appropriate pages. Scanning them, I found the information I needed. In both the Rouen and Paris traditions, the king of spades represented the biblical king David. I shut the book and put it back in the bag with the other books I had bought.

I puzzled over it as I walked back into the living. "King David," I told Sophie and Marylou as I resumed my seat on the sofa.

"David?" Marylou and Sophie said in unison. We all stared at one another.

"What does that mean?" Marylou asked after a moment.

"I'm not sure," I said. "All I can think of is the story of David and Bathsheba."

"And how David had Bathsheba's husband sent into the front lines of the battle, knowing he would probably be killed, and then David could have her for himself," Sophie said.

"Exactly."

Marylou frowned. "You're forgetting part of the story. David got Bathsheba pregnant while she was still married to her husband, Uriah the Hittite. She was the mother of Solomon."

"This is all giving me a headache," Sophie said with a grimace.

"Me, too." I sighed. "But before we go any further with this, we need to let Deputy Ainsworth know about it." I got up from the sofa and went to the phone. I dialed the operator and asked for the room where the sheriff's department was working.

Someone answered eventually. I identified myself and asked for Deputy Ainsworth. The first response was that he was too busy at the moment to talk to me. I insisted that what I had to tell him was of vital significance to the investigation—I hoped I wasn't lying about that—and the man on the other end gave in.

I had to wait about a minute, but Deputy Ainsworth came on the line. "Yes, what is it?" His voice was terse to the point of rudeness.

I identified myself again. "I'm sorry to bother you, Deputy, but I've found something in our suite that I think could be important evidence. I think you really need to come see it, and as soon as possible."

"What is it?" he asked.

"It's another playing card. Just come up and look at it," I told him. "I'll explain when you get here. It really is important."

I heard some muttering. "Okay, look, I'm in the middle of something, and I can't leave it. Give me about twenty minutes." The phone clicked in my ear.

"He's coming up in about twenty minutes. He's in

the middle of something," I said while putting the receiver in its cradle. "So we'll just have to wait."

"I bet he was annoyed." Sophie grinned.

"Yes," I said. "I know he thinks I'm probably one of those women who's so desperate for attention that she manufactures reasons to call the police."

"He'll see differently when he gets here," Marylou said, "and then he'll be sorry he didn't come right away."

"Let's hope so," I said. I sat down on the sofa and stared at the card lying on the cushion next to me.

"That bloodstain must mean this card was part of the deck Avery Trowbridge was playing with," I said. "But how did it get blood on it if it was lying on the table with the other cards? I don't remember seeing any blood on the table, just on Avery himself and the chair." I shuddered as an all-too-graphic image flashed through my brain.

"He had to have been holding it," Sophie said.

"Was he holding two cards, do you think?" Marylou asked.

I shrugged. "He could have been, and then someone removed this one from his hand. Or someone replaced this card with the queen of diamonds."

"To implicate someone else in the murder," Sophie said.

"That's what I think," I said. "The question is, exactly whom does this card implicate?"

"David also slew the giant Goliath," Marylou said. She stopped, frowning.

Sophie and I looked at her, waiting for her to continue.

"Avery was a giant, in a way," Marylou said. "At least in the bridge world. Maybe he was killed because someone wanted the giant out of his way."

"So the other person could become the giant," I said.

"Basil," Sophie said. "What do you want to bet that Avery was the person who would have taken over that bridge column if he hadn't been killed?"

"It's a possibility," I said. "And if that's the case, then someone switched the card in Avery's hand to protect Basil and shift the suspicion onto someone else, namely Lorraine."

"And that means Paula," Marylou said. "But when could she have done it? Didn't she come into the room after you had found the body?"

"Yes," I said, thinking it through. "She *came into the room*, as you said. But where was she before that? I thought she entered from the corridor outside, but what if she was in the bedroom instead? I had my back to the rest of the suite. She could have come from the bedroom, and I didn't realize it at the time."

"The door to the suite was open just a little bit when you walked by," Sophie said.

"It was," I agreed. "I suppose Paula could have opened it, and it was just bad luck that I happened to come in while she was in the other room. If that's the case, she was foolish not to be sure the door was shut behind her."

"Or she could have found the door open, too, and then when she went in to see Avery, she found him dead," Marylou said.

"That, too," I said. "Either way, I think she was already in Avery's suite when I went in."

"And she switched the cards." Marylou shook her head, still having trouble believing that Paula could have done it.

I jumped up from the couch and went back to the phone. Sophie and Marylou watched me, startled, but they didn't say anything. I dialed the operator again.

I was acting on impulse, but it might just pay off. I couldn't stop thinking about the story of David and Goliath. "Haskell Crenshaw's room," I said when the operator answered.

I crossed my fingers, hoping he would be in his room. If not, I would have him paged. The phone rang four times, and I figured it was about to go to voice mail when it was picked up.

"Hello." The voice sounded groggy.

"Mr. Crenshaw?"

He cleared his throat and in a more alert tone said, "Yes, who is it?"

"Emma Diamond," I said. "Look, I don't have time to explain right now, but it's really urgent that I talk to you. Can you come up to my suite right away?" I gave him the suite number.

"What do you want?" He sounded very annoyed and slightly drunk. "Why should I talk to you? Who are you again?"

I gave him my name and reminded him where we had met. "This is about Avery Trowbridge's murder, and it's very important," I said. "Please just come, and I'll explain when you get here."

"What's the room number again?"

Good, I had obviously got his attention. I gave him the number a second time, and he said he would be right along. He was one floor down from us.

I replaced the phone on its cradle and came back to the sofa. As I sat down, Sophie asked, "So what was all that about?"

"David and Goliath," I said. Sophie got it, but Marylou continued to look puzzled.

"If Avery was Goliath," Sophie explained, "then his business manager would know a lot about his career."

"And he could say whether Avery was the one who was going to be doing the bridge column," Marylou said. "And anything else the killer might want to take over, once Goliath was dead."

"Exactly," Sophie and I said in unison.

A knock came at the door, and Sophie went to answer it. Haskell Crenshaw strode in, looking slightly the worse for drink. He had made an attempt at combing his hair, but stray tufts stuck out at odd angles. His clothes had obviously been slept in, and his eyes were bloodshot.

"Thank you for coming so quickly, Mr. Crenshaw," I said. "Please, have a seat." I indicated a place on the sofa. Using the tissue, I had stuck the king of spades back in its hiding place when I heard him knock on the door.

"You said something about Avery's murder," Crenshaw said. He blinked at me.

Sophie left the room, and I figured she was going to make some coffee. Crenshaw could definitely use it.

"Yes," I said. "This has to do with Avery's murder."

"What's it to you?" Crenshaw said. He flapped a hand in the air. "Why are you ladies so interested? It's got nothing to do with you."

"In a way, it has," I said. "I was the one who found him."

"Oh." That sobered him a bit. He turned his head away for a moment. When he faced me again, he appeared more alert. "Why do you want to talk to me? I didn't kill him. And you're not the police."

"No, we're not," I said, smiling in an attempt to placate him. "But we're involved, unfortunately. I think you can help get this solved. You want to find Avery's killer, don't you?"

Crenshaw nodded, still wary.

"You were Avery Trowbridge's business manager," I said.

He nodded again.

"He fired you, though, didn't he?"

"How do you know that?" Crenshaw asked, scowling at me.

I thought he would have denied it, and I was a bit surprised. Maybe his brain was still clouded by sleep, or alcohol, or both. "I overheard part of a conversation," I said. "Next door."

Crenshaw thought about that a moment. Then enlightenment dawned. "Yeah, Avery was like that. He fired me several times, but he always hired me back in a day or two. It never bothered me, because I always knew we'd patch things up. Avery needed me as much as I needed him."

"Okay," I said. "So you were back in Avery's good graces before he was killed?"

"Yes," Crenshaw said. "We made up that night." He sighed. "God, I'm going to miss him." He turned away for a moment. He pulled a wrinkled handkerchief from his pocket and wiped his eyes.

I felt a pang of sympathy for Crenshaw. I had begun to think he really cared deeply about Avery, in more than a professional sense. He seemed to be the only person mourning the dead man, except for his son.

"I know this is hard for you," I said, "and I regret that. But I think you know something that could be really important in this case."

"What?" Crenshaw said. He tucked the handkerchief back in his pocket.

"We heard something interesting a little while ago," I said. "Something involving Basil Dumont."

Crenshaw snorted. "That weenie! Avery hated him.

And that god-awful wife of his. I don't know why Avery got mixed up with Paula. She's nuts."

"Basil and Paula are going to remarry," I said.

"They deserve each other," Crenshaw said.

Sophie came back and sat down. She held up five fingers, and I took that to mean that the coffee would be ready in about five minutes. I nodded before turning back to Crenshaw.

"They had some other news to share," I said. "Apparently Basil has been asked to take over a nationally syndicated bridge column."

"The hell he has!" Crenshaw half rose from his spot on the sofa. He cursed briefly as he sat down again. "That was going to be Avery's gig. The little creep must have called them the minute he knew Avery was dead." Slowly, comprehension dawned on his face.

Sophie, Marylou, and I exchanged glances.

"The bastard!" Crenshaw shouted, and then he startled us all by slamming a fist against the table beside the sofa so hard it fell over. "He killed Avery, the sonofabitch. I'll rip his goddamn head off."

Chapter 26

For a moment I was afraid Haskell Crenshaw would run out of the room in search of Basil Dumont. He was a big, powerful man, and if he managed to get his hands on Dumont, there probably wouldn't be too much left of the smaller man.

"Calm down, and don't you dare get up from that sofa."

Marylou rarely raised her voice or spoke in such a sharp, commanding tone, but when she did, the person to whom it was directed usually didn't argue. The expression on Haskell Crenshaw's face was almost comical. He subsided on the couch without a word, shocked into silence, for the moment at least.

"That's better," Marylou said, her voice resuming its normal placid tone. "There's no need for any of that. Whoever the killer is, I'm sure the sheriff's department is more than capable of dealing with him or her."

"I guess you're right," Crenshaw muttered. He rubbed his forehead as if his head ached.

I had noticed Sophie slipping out of the room when Marylou spoke, and now she returned with a cup of coffee for Crenshaw. "Drink this," she told him. "This will help."

Crenshaw stared at her for a moment, but he accepted the cup. He sipped from it, then grimaced. "There's no sugar in it."

"Drink it anyway," Sophie said. "It will do you good." Her tone and her stance brooked no opposition to her instructions.

"Deputy Ainsworth will be here any minute now," I said, watching Crenshaw as I spoke. "We can tell him our suspicions about Basil Dumont, and he can take it from there."

Crenshaw nodded. "You're right. I was just letting my temper get away from me. I can't stand the thought that that weenie is alive and trying to take over Avery's gigs. It burns the hell out of me that he might get away with it."

"We all certainly appreciate your loyalty to your client," Marylou said.

"He was more than that," Crenshaw said, his voice soft. He pressed his handkerchief to his eyes again.

A knock on the door ended what could have become an increasingly awkward interlude. Sophie jumped up from her chair and almost ran to the door. She held it open for Deputy Ainsworth and his subordinate, Deputy Jordan, to enter.

"Ladies," Ainsworth said, nodding at us. "Mr. Crenshaw." We all nodded back at him.

"You said you had something to show me, Mrs. Diamond?" Ainsworth stared at me, and I wanted to squirm like a guilty child.

I had been thinking about what to do and say when Ainsworth appeared. For the moment, I didn't think anyone else should know about the card I had found.

I wanted Haskell Crenshaw out of the room when I revealed the king of spades to Ainsworth. The fewer people who knew about it, the better—that was my reasoning.

"Yes," I said, "but before we get to that, we have something we think you should know. Mr. Crenshaw can explain the significance of it."

Crenshaw shot me an odd look before he addressed the deputy. "These ladies told me that Basil Dumont has been asked to take over a nationally syndicated bridge column. He made that announcement to them a little earlier today."

Ainsworth appeared to be hanging on to his temper by a thread. "Why is that important?"

Crenshaw breathed deeply before answering. "Avery Trowbridge was all set to take over that column. They were going to fax the contracts right here to the hotel. Today, as a matter of fact."

I was watching Ainsworth's face closely while he spoke to Crenshaw, and at the word "fax," Ainsworth cut a glance sideways at his subordinate, Deputy Jordan, who stood near him in his line of sight. I followed his gaze, and I saw Jordan nod, almost imperceptibly.

Ainsworth's eyes focused on Crenshaw. "So you're trying to tell me that Mr. Dumont might have killed Trowbridge so he could take over this column?" He didn't sound quite as surprised as I would have expected.

Crenshaw stood up and stepped forward a few paces, until he was only two feet away from the deputy. "I don't think you understand what was at stake here, Deputy. Avery Trowbridge was a big name in the bridge world, and he was only going to get bigger once he was writing this column. It's read all over the world. It gives whoever writes it a very high profile, and that leads to a lot of lucrative gigs. Avery was going to start making even more money once his name was on that column."

"You would have, too, wouldn't you?" Ainsworth asked.

Crenshaw nodded. "Yes, I would have."

"That makes it sound more plausible," Ainsworth said.

"You're damn right it's plausible," Crenshaw responded, the heat rising in his voice. "That weenie Dumont never could compete with Avery—alive, that is. With Avery out of the way, the field is clear now. He got tired of always being second choice, and that's why he killed Avery. The minute Avery was dead, he must have called the syndicate to offer his services, but I'll bet you he didn't tell them Avery was murdered."

"This will certainly bear investigating," Ainsworth said. "I appreciate the information, Mr. Crenshaw. Do you have anything more to add to it?"

Crenshaw shook his head. "No, that's it, I guess."

"Right," Ainsworth said. "Then perhaps you'll excuse me while I talk to these ladies. And don't talk about what you've told me to anyone. Don't go anywhere near Mr. Dumont, either." He stared hard at Crenshaw to emphasize his point.

Crenshaw paled slightly. "Sure," he said. He moved around Ainsworth toward the door. "Thanks for the coffee, ladies." He opened the door and disappeared through it, closing it softly behind him.

Ainsworth turned his attention to me. "Now, Mrs. Diamond, what was it you wanted to show me that you didn't want Crenshaw to see?"

I gave the deputy a brief smile before I stood up from the sofa. "It's right here," I said, turning slightly and pointing downward at the space between the cushion and the arm of the sofa.

Deputy Jordan stepped forward and peered down as I moved aside. She grasped the cushion and pulled it up, setting it down on top of the other cushion. The card fell over, faceup, and the deputy stared at it for a moment.

"It's a card, sir," she said, turning to face her superior. "The king of spades."

Ainsworth frowned. "When you called me, you said it was about a playing card. So why is this card so important?"

"Someone hid it in our sofa, and it's got what looks like blood on it," I said.

Without saying another word, Jordan pulled out her cell phone and punched in a number. When someone answered, she requested a crime scene technician to come collect some evidence.

Ainsworth walked over to the sofa and squatted to get a better look at the card.

"That does look like a possible bloodstain," he said as he stood up. "Did any of you touch it?"

"I did," I said, "before I realized it could be evidence. After that, I handled it with a tissue."

"Did one of you put it here?" Ainsworth stared at each of us in turn.

"Certainly not," Marylou said with a big frown.

"Of course not," Sophie said.

"No," I said, "but we think we know who did."

"And that would be?" Ainsworth arched an eyebrow at me.

"Paula Trowbridge," I said, "when she was here yesterday morning with Marylou."

"She was alone once for a couple of minutes,"

Marylou said. "She could have done it then, I suppose."

"But to be fair," Sophie said, with a quick glance at me, "someone with a passkey could have come in here and put it in the sofa."

Ainsworth didn't respond to that gambit. He started to speak, but a knock at the door interrupted him.

Deputy Jordan went to the door and admitted a fellow officer. She brought him over to the sofa and explained the situation. First, he took some pictures with a digital camera. Putting away the camera, he pulled on a pair of thin cotton gloves, picked the card up by pressing his fingers against two edges of the card, and dropped the king of spades into a clear envelope. He labeled the envelope with a marker. He conferred in undertones with Jordan near the door to the suite before exiting.

We had waited in silence until he was gone.

"Have you counted the cards that were on the table next door?"

Ainsworth stared at me for a moment before turning to Jordan. "Well?" was all he said.

"No, sir," Jordan replied. "I don't think they've been counted. But I'll make sure they are now."

Ainsworth nodded at her, and she left the suite, presumably to count the cards herself or oversee it.

"I'm sure you must have a theory about that card," Ainsworth said, addressing me.

"Yes," I said, "but this is going to take a little while." Deputy Jordan must not have passed along my information about the history of playing cards. That was annoying, but I couldn't waste time now being irritated.

Ainsworth shook his head, but before he spoke, I

held up a hand. "I know you're extremely busy, Deputy, but this is really very important. Please, sit down, and let me explain."

He didn't roll his eyes, but I figured he must have wanted to. Instead, he replaced the sofa cushion, motioned for me to take a seat, and sat down once I was seated.

"Go ahead," he said.

"I bought a book about the history of bridge," I said, and I could see the deputy's eyes beginning to glaze over. "There's a section on the history of playing cards, and who the face cards represent."

He perked up at that. He nodded.

"I won't give you the long version," I said. I explained the two systems and the names of the various persons each card represented. The whole time I talked, Marylou and Sophie watched the deputy closely, with the occasional glance at me.

"So the queen of diamonds could mean Rachel," Ainsworth said. "Jacob's second wife, right?"

"Yes," I said.

"And that could mean Paula Trowbridge."

"Yes," I said again.

"Who is this Argine?" Ainsworth asked.

"They're really not sure," I said, "but it could be an anagram of the Latin word for 'queen,' *regina*." I paused for a moment. "I found out today that Lorraine Trowbridge's middle name is Regina, and according to her son, Avery used it as kind of a nickname for her."

"Basically, then, if what you say about the card is right, Trowbridge was trying to tell us one of his wives killed him," Ainsworth said. "I suppose it's possible. We know he didn't die immediately. He might have been able to pick up a card."

His cell phone rang, and he got up from the sofa.

"Excuse me, ladies." He strode over to a corner of the room to answer the call.

We could hear him speaking, but the words were unintelligible, the conversation brief. He snapped his phone shut and returned to the sofa.

"There were only fifty-one cards at the crime scene," Ainsworth said, "counting the one in the victim's hand."

"So it looks like the king of spades came from the same deck," Sophie said.

"Yeah," Ainsworth said, "it sure looks like it." He turned to me. "So what about the king of spades?"

"King David," I said promptly.

"And that means?" Ainsworth was clearly puzzled.

"Think of David and Bathsheba," I said. "Or David and Goliath." I waited, wondering whether Ainsworth would draw the same conclusions that we had.

Marylou started to speak, but I held up my hand. She subsided, nodding.

"David and Bathsheba," the deputy said. "Paula Trowbridge was married to Basil Dumont before she married Trowbridge, right?"

"Yes," I said.

"So maybe Dumont wanted to kill Trowbridge for taking his wife away from him. Is that what you're saying?"

"It's a possibility," I said, "but I don't think that's really the motive."

"David and Goliath, then," Ainsworth said. "Trowbridge was Goliath, because he had a bigger name in the bridge world. David is Dumont, who was jealous and wanted to take his place. David the giant killer. Dumont."

I could see that this line of reasoning appealed to him.

"Okay, then," Ainsworth said, "if the king of spades is supposed to point the finger at Dumont, how did it get in here?"

"I've thought about that," I said, "and I think what happened is this. When I went into the room next door, I think Paula Trowbridge was already in there, in the bedroom. She might have heard me and hid. She found the body before I did, saw that Avery was holding the king of spades in his hand. She knew what he was trying to tell us, and she put the queen of diamonds in his hand instead, to throw suspicion on someone else."

"Even herself?" Ainsworth cocked an eyebrow in skepticism.

"I doubt she thought of it that way," I said.

"I'm sure she didn't," Marylou said. "Paula must have been thinking of the queen as Argine, the anagram of *regina*. She certainly would have known that Lorraine's middle name is Regina, and that Avery used it as a nickname for his first wife."

"That makes sense," Ainsworth said, nodding. "And it's plausible, I guess, that Paula Trowbridge could have been in the room before you got there."

I nodded. "I heard her behind me, but I couldn't swear she came into the room from the hall. The more I've thought about it, the more I really do think she was in the bedroom. She simply waited until my back was to her before she came up to me, pretending she had just come into the suite."

"This sure is a crazy case," Ainsworth said, shaking his head.

"I suppose we've made it more complicated," I said, "telling you all this about the meaning of the cards, and so on."

Ainsworth laughed. "Yeah, you have, but I wouldn't

have known anything about it if you hadn't told me. It's weird, but I'm danged if I don't believe you're right. It all has to mean something. The question is, how do I know which interpretation is the right one?"

Before Sophie, Marylou, or I could respond to him, someone banged loudly on our door. Once again, Sophie went to answer it. She barely had time to step out of the way before Paula Trowbridge pushed the door so hard it banged against the doorstop and shuddered there. Paula strode into the room, Basil Dumont in tow. He didn't look too happy to be here.

"What on earth?" Marylou said, standing up. "Paula, what is the matter with you? You could have hurt Sophie."

Paula didn't pay Marylou the least attention. She focused on Ainsworth. She got right up in his face and said, "I want you to go arrest that man right this minute. He tried to kill Basil, and if I hadn't been there, he would have!"

Chapter 27

"What man are you talking about?" Ainsworth remained immobile as he stared down at Paula.

"Haskell Crenshaw," Paula said, breathing heavily from the combination of anger and exertion. "Who else? That man had the nerve to attack Basil, and I want you to arrest him for attempted murder."

We all stared at Basil Dumont, who flushed under our scrutiny. As far as I could tell, he wasn't hurt. He wasn't bleeding or clutching any part of his anatomy in pain. Perhaps his pride was aching, but that was about all.

"Ma'am, Mr. Dumont looks okay to me," Ainsworth said in a placatory tone. "Mr. Dumont, did Mr. Crenshaw strike you?"

"No, Officer," Dumont said. "He didn't lay a hand on me."

Ainsworth regarded Paula stonily, and after a moment, Paula had the grace to blush. "Maybe I was a little excited," she said, "but Crenshaw did threaten Basil. I heard him."

"Did he threaten you, Mr. Dumont?" Ainsworth addressed the alleged victim.

Dumont sighed. "All he said was that he wasn't

going to let me get away with it. Then he called me a few nasty names, and that was the extent of it."

"He said he'd see you in hell." Paula poked Dumont on the arm. "Don't forget that part. That sounds like a death threat to me."

"I'll have a word with Mr. Crenshaw," Ainsworth said. "I'm sure he won't accost you again, Mr. Dumont."

"Thank you, Deputy," Dumont said. Paula scowled but didn't say anything.

"I do have some questions for you, Mr. Dumont," Ainsworth said. "Would you mind accompanying me downstairs?"

"What kind of questions?" Paula's voice held a note of panic, and I regarded her with interest. "Basil has already told you everything he knows."

"I'd rather be the judge of that, Mrs. Trowbridge." Ainsworth was making an obvious effort to remain polite, but I wondered how much longer he could manage if Paula kept on being, well, Paula. As usual, she was oblivious to the effect she was having on the deputy.

"I should add," Ainsworth continued, "that I also have some questions for you, Mrs. Trowbridge, so you can both come along with me downstairs, all right?"

Paula blanched. "I don't have anything else to tell you either, Deputy. But if you insist on talking to me, I want you to do it right here. I want my friends with me." Her mouth set in mulish lines. Ainsworth was in for a struggle with her, the mood she seemed to be in right now.

"Now, Paula," Dumont said, "don't be silly. Let's just go downstairs and talk to the deputy like he asks. We don't have anything to worry about."

Indeed, he appeared perfectly calm. Paula was the

one who seemed to be having some kind of break-down. She stared at Dumont, tears beginning to pud-dle in her eyes. "Oh, Basil," she said, launching herself at him.

She almost knocked him over, but he wrapped his arms around her and steadied them both. As Paula sobbed on his shoulder, he stared helplessly at the rest of us.

No one spoke for a moment. Then Marylou said, "Basil, why don't you get Paula settled on the sofa, and I'll get her something to drink." She glanced at Ainsworth, and he nodded permission. He didn't look very happy with the situation, though.

Nodding, Basil steered Paula toward the sofa, and she made no effort to stop him. He lowered her onto a cushion and sat down beside her. She threw her arms around his neck and continued sobbing against his shoulder.

Marylou had left the room, and she came back with about half a small glass of amber liquid. "Here, Paula, drink this." She tapped Paula on the shoulder.

Paula sobbed a moment longer, but with Dumont's gentle insistence, she released her hold on him and turned to Marylou. "What is it?" she asked as she accepted the glass.

"A little brandy," Marylou said. "It will do you good."

Paula tossed back the brandy in one gulp, and she gasped as she handed the glass back to Marylou.

"Thank you," Paula said, her voice a bit hoarse. "I guess I needed that."

"What on *earth* is the matter with you?" Dumont asked her, peering at her with a mingled look of alarm and distaste.

Paula didn't answer. She stared mutely back at him.

Dumont regarded her for a moment; then comprehension dawned in his face. He jumped up from the sofa and turned to stare down at her.

"My God," he said, "I don't believe it. You think I killed Avery, don't you?"

Paula still didn't respond, and Dumont gazed wildly at the rest of us. "She's crazy," he said, his voice beginning to resemble the bleating of a sheep. "She's absolutely freaking nuts. I didn't kill Avery. How could you even think such a thing?"

Ainsworth was watching the developing scene with considerable interest. I guessed he was letting it play out to see what could be gleaned from it. He might get more from Dumont and Paula here than he would in a one-on-one session in the office downstairs.

Dumont continued to look from one to the other of us, seeking our reassurance, I supposed, that Paula really was nuts for thinking he was the killer. The problem was, of course, that Marylou, Sophie, and I agreed with Paula. The damning evidence of the king of spades put him at the head of the list. He certainly had a lot to gain from Avery Trowbridge's death, perhaps more than anyone else.

"Mr. Dumont, is it true that you are going to be writing a nationally syndicated bridge column?" Ainsworth finally spoke, and Dumont jerked in surprise.

"Why, um, yes," Dumont said. He swallowed, and sweat began to form on his brow. "I, um, just found out about it." He stared at the deputy.

"Is it also true that Avery Trowbridge was going to write that column instead of you?"

Dumont licked his lips. For a moment he seemed unable to speak. "Uh, well, I guess so." The sweat streamed down his face now. He mopped at it ineffectually with his hands.

"How did you get the job so quickly?" Ainsworth continued to stare at Dumont, and Dumont seemed to wilt further.

"Um, I guess I called the syndicate when I heard Avery was dead," Dumont said. He gave up trying to keep the sweat off his face. If he didn't stop sweating soon, he would completely dehydrate himself.

Sophie, Marylou, and I watched with unabashed interest. Ainsworth could stop this at any moment and take Dumont and Paula downstairs, but I didn't think he wanted to break the rising tension in the room.

Paula sat, head in hands, on the sofa. She had stopped crying, but her labored breathing was evidence of her distress.

"This syndicate offered you the job right away then?" Ainsworth asked.

"Oh, yes, they were quite happy I was able to take it over," Dumont said, something like relief in his voice. "I was on their short list anyway, and they're perfectly happy with me."

"It's a lucky break for you," Ainsworth said in an encouraging tone.

"Oh, yes, it is," Dumont said, a tentative smile on his face. "It's the break I've been waiting for. For years."

Paula groaned, and Dumont's face fell. It hit him then, what Ainsworth had been leading up to.

"I didn't kill Avery," he said, once again sounding like a sheep. "I wanted to write the column, but not bad enough to kill someone. Surely you can't believe I'd do something like that?"

"I'm sure you can see how it looks to me," Ainsworth said, his voice smooth as silk. "It sounds like a very good motive to me."

Dumont was sweating even more now, and I was

afraid he would pass out from fear alone. He trembled as he sank down on the sofa beside Paula. "Oh my God," he said, "this is a nightmare." He stared at Paula. His eyes closed briefly, and a moment later he sighed, as if he had come to some decision.

"I didn't kill Avery," Dumont said. The sheep was gone. His voice firm, he continued. "I couldn't have killed Avery. I have an alibi for the whole night."

Paula's head jerked up. "Oh, Basil, don't. Don't lie." She reached toward him.

Dumont shied away from her. "It's not a lie, Paula. You're not going to like what I'm going to say, but it's the truth, I swear to God."

"What is your alibi, Mr. Dumont?" Ainsworth asked.

Basil licked his lips before replying. "I spent the whole night with someone. A woman. We were never out of each other's sight the whole night long. I swear it."

"Who is the woman?" Ainsworth asked.

Dumont hesitated. "I suppose I have no choice. It was Lorraine. Lorraine Trowbridge."

That wasn't very gallant of him, I thought. At the very least, he could have insisted on talking to the deputy in private.

Paula howled with rage, and she started beating Dumont with her fists. Ainsworth stepped in quickly and pulled her away from Dumont before she could inflict too much damage. One of her fists had connected with his right eye, though, and he would probably have a nice shiner as a result.

"Mrs. Trowbridge, calm down," Ainsworth said in a stern voice. He held Paula in a tight grasp. She struggled for a moment before subsiding weakly in the deputy's arms.

Marylou came forward and took Paula from the

deputy. She led Paula to her own chair and sat her down in it. Paula clutched at Marylou's hand and held on to it.

Ainsworth faced Dumont, who had a hand over his right eye. "I suppose Mrs. Trowbridge will back you up, Mr. Dumont?"

Dumont nodded.

Of course she will, I thought. She needed an alibi, too. For a moment, I was tempted to think that Dumont had made up the whole thing, but as I watched him, I came to the conclusion that he was telling the truth. He was so relieved that I didn't think he was faking it.

"You're sure that neither of you left the other one alone, even for a few minutes, that night?"

Dumont stared up at the deputy. "I'm sure." He blushed. "We were, um, quite busy until early in the morning."

Paula howled again, and Marylou held on to her. All the fight seemed to have gone out of Paula, though, and she just sat there in the chair.

"I did it all for nothing," she said, her voice hoarse with emotion. "You sorry sonofabitch. I thought I was protecting you, and all the time you were screwing that bitch behind my back." She breathed heavily for a moment. "You were going to marry me as soon as Avery and I got a divorce."

"How were you protecting *me*?" Dumont said. "I didn't kill Avery."

"I found Avery before Emma did," Paula said. She stared blankly ahead of her. "He had a card in his hand. The king of spades. I thought he was trying to say that you had killed him."

"With the bloody king of spades?" Dumont was

clearly incredulous. "Why the hell would you think he meant me?"

"David, the king of spades," Paula said. "David, who killed Goliath. David, the puny little man who slew the great giant." The acid fairly spewed from her mouth as she said the words "puny little man," and Dumont flinched.

"So I took that card, and put the queen of diamonds in his hand instead," Paula continued. "Then I heard footsteps in the corridor, and I went into Avery's bedroom to hide. That's when Emma came in. I pretended I came in from the corridor, and that she was the one who found the body."

"And at some point, when you were here with Marylou and Sophie," I said, "you hid the card in our sofa."

Paula nodded. "I was planning to retrieve it later and destroy it. I guess I wasn't thinking too clearly."

"You tampered with a crime scene," Ainsworth said. "I may have to charge you with that."

Paula shrugged. "It doesn't matter. I don't care anymore." She glared at Dumont.

"Now, Paula," Marylou said, "don't talk like that. It's a good thing you found out what a rat Basil is, so that you didn't make the mistake of marrying him again." She glared at Dumont, too, and he flushed and turned away.

"I think you had both better come downstairs with me," Ainsworth said. "I want to take your statements down, and I'll have to decide whether to charge you, Mrs. Trowbridge."

Paula and Dumont stood up. Ainsworth escorted them to the door. They preceded him into the hallway. He paused at the door to look back at Sophie, Marylou, and me. "I'll be back to talk to you ladies later." With that, the door shut behind him.

"Oh my goodness," Marylou said, sinking down on the sofa in the spot vacated by Basil Dumont. "Did you ever in your life see such a scene?"

"Sure," Sophie said, "every day on the soap operas." She shook her head. "What a mess."

I nodded, thinking about the implications of what had taken place. "You realize, don't you, that if Dumont's alibi holds up, then neither he nor Lorraine Trowbridge killed Avery?"

"Yes," Sophie said, "and that leaves Paula."

"What about Will Trowbridge?" Marylou said.

"Will didn't kill his father," I said.

"How can you be so sure?" Sophie asked. "I know you think he's a nice young man, Emma, but nice young men have killed their fathers before."

"I know that," I said, "but while everything was going on, I was thinking about David."

"David?" Marylou and Sophie asked at the same time.

"David," I said. "There's another story about David that we didn't think about."

Chapter 28

I waited a moment to see whether Sophie or Marylou realized the story I meant.

Sophie got it first. "David and Jonathan."

Marylou looked bewildered for a moment. "David and Jonathan," she said slowly. "Oh."

I nodded. "Yes, exactly."

Marylou frowned. "David and Jonathan were really good friends. They loved each other, but what has that got to do with anything?"

Ordinarily Marylou wasn't this dense. Sophie and I exchanged glances.

"Not everybody believes the relationship between David and Jonathan was platonic," Sophie said.

"Yes," I said, "some scholars think they could have been lovers."

"I've never heard that," Marylou said, surprise evident on her face. "Are you sure?"

Over the years I've attended a number of lectures on various topics with my brother, Jake, and his partner, Luke. Several of them had to do with the Bible and homosexuality. "Yes, I'm sure," I said. "Look, no one will ever really know, but that doesn't really matter so much in this case."

"Jonathan was an older man who loved a younger man, David," Sophie said. She had attended some of the lectures as well. "Avery Trowbridge was older than Haskell Crenshaw, and we know that they were lovers. Maybe Avery picked up. the king of spades, the David card, to point the finger at *his* 'David.'"

Marylou shook her head. "Well, I guess that makes as much sense as any of the other interpretations we've heard."

"It sure does," Sophie said. "And we know Crenshaw had a motive."

"I think he was in love with Avery," I said, thinking back on Crenshaw's behavior. "Think about the way he was killed, too. Stabbed in the chest."

"A crime of passion," Marylou said, and Sophie and I nodded.

"Exactly. The act of a jealous lover," Sophie said.

"And maybe the act of a man who was being pushed out of his lover's life," I said.

"What do you mean?" Marylou asked.

"We know that Avery had fired Crenshaw, right?" I asked. They both nodded. "We have only Crenshaw's word for it that they made up after the fight. For all we know, they *didn't* make up."

"So Crenshaw would have lost out on all the money about to come Avery's way with the bridge column, besides being cut out of Avery's life as his lover." Sophie nodded emphatically. "Yes, that has to be it."

"I guess you're right," Marylou said, "But how could you prove something like that? Unless Avery confirmed with someone else that he had fired Crenshaw, permanently, then there's no evidence that he did it."

"And the case seems to rest on that," Sophie said.

"There might *be* evidence, for all we know," I said,

not ready to admit defeat. "Ainsworth just has to know where to look. Frankly, I doubt if this would be the only evidence, anyway. There's bound to be something else. Blood on the killer's clothes, fibers, who knows what?"

"You're right," Sophie said, brightening.

"I guess this means you think Veronica Hinkelmeier is out of the picture," Marylou said.

"Unfortunately, yes," Sophie said. "I wish it was her. Somebody ought to lock her up for something."

"I don't think there's much hope of that, but surely by now the owners have got wind of some of her behavior. That ought to be enough for them to consider firing her." I said.

"I sure feel sorry for her daughter," Marylou said, and Sophie and I agreed.

"So what are we going to do now?" Marylou asked.

"We have to tell all this to Ainsworth," I said, "and after that, it's out of our hands."

"Yes," Sophie said. "And frankly, I'll be glad when it's all over."

"Me, too," Marylou said.

I would, too, though frankly I felt sorry for everyone involved in the case. Avery Trowbridge had caused all kinds of trouble for those around him, and I thought it terribly sad that none of them had a happy relationship. Most of them were unpleasant people, and perhaps I shouldn't extend my sympathies too far. I felt most deeply for Will Trowbridge. He seemed like a decent young man, and I hoped he would get through this somehow without being horribly scarred emotionally.

"Didn't Ainsworth say he would talk to us later?" Sophie asked.

"Yes," I said.

"So do you think that means he's planning to come back here?"

"I would think so," I told her. I got up and went to the phone. "We might as well find out for sure, though." I punched 0 for the operator. I asked for the room the sheriff's department was using, and moments later a woman answered.

I identified myself and asked for Ainsworth.

"This is Deputy Jordan, Mrs. Diamond," she said. "Actually, I believe Deputy Ainsworth is on his way to your suite already. He should be there any minute now."

"Thank you," I said, and hung up the phone. "He's already on his way," I told Marylou and Sophie.

I had barely finished speaking when someone knocked on the door. Motioning for Sophie to remain seated, I went to answer the knock.

"Come in, Deputy," I said, stepping aside to let Ainsworth enter the room.

"We're glad you came back so quickly," Sophie said, grinning at him, "because we've figured it out, and we couldn't wait to tell you."

Ainsworth smiled at her. He waited for me to sit down; then he sat at the other end of the sofa. "Let me guess," he said. "You finally remembered the story of David and Jonathan."

The look on Sophie's face was priceless, and Marylou and I couldn't help laughing.

"Go ahead and laugh," she said crossly. "I should have realized you would remember that story, too." She tossed her hair back, and Ainsworth's eyes gleamed with appreciation.

"I'm not really trying to upstage you," Ainsworth said, smiling, "because, to be honest, I was already ahead of you on that one. The David and Jonathan angle was just another pointer."

"Really?" I asked. "So you already suspected Crenshaw?"

"Yes," Ainsworth said. "We knew the victim had fired him as a business manager and agent. Of course, at first Crenshaw told us that he and the victim had patched things up, and that he wasn't fired after all."

"But that turned out to be a lie," I said when the deputy paused.

"Exactly," Ainsworth replied. "We checked the phone calls that the victim received here at the hotel, including any faxes. He received a fax the night he was killed, and that put a different spin on everything."

"Come on, now, don't keep us in suspense," Sophie said, tossing her hair.

Ainsworth remained silent for a moment, enjoying the view. "Right. Well, that fax originated from a number in New York. We found out that the number belonged to an agency, and when we called the agency, we discovered that they had faxed a contract to Trowbridge. And what really clinched it: he had signed it and faxed it back immediately."

"So he had signed with a new agent," I said.

"And Crenshaw knew it," Marylou said.

"I believe so," Ainsworth replied.

"Have you arrested him yet?" I asked.

Ainsworth shook his head. "Not yet, no. I'm still waiting on a couple of bits of information, but I don't think we'll have any problem. Proving that he did it, that is. I can't really say any more than that. In fact, I probably shouldn't have said this much, but you were actually a big help in some ways." He grinned at me.

"Thanks," I said, smiling in return. In truth I actually felt a little embarrassed. We really had been pretty nosy, inserting ourselves into this investigation, and we were lucky that Ainsworth had taken such a tolerant attitude to our "help."

"There's still one thing that puzzles me," I said. "Why didn't Crenshaw call my room to let me know the bridge lesson was canceled? He called Bob and Bart."

Ainsworth laughed. "It was a mistake on Trowbridge's part. He transposed two of the numbers. Someone else got the message you should have received. We traced the calls to one of the house phones in the lobby."

I shook my head in wonder. Such a simple answer to a question that had made me rather uncomfortable.

Once again, someone knocked at the door. This time Marylou got up to answer it. Ainsworth stood up, preparing to taking his leave of us.

"Mr. Crenshaw," Marylou said. "Um, won't you come in?" The strain was evident in her voice. Sophie and I exchanged startled looks.

Haskell Crenshaw walked into the room. He halted when he spotted Ainsworth. He smiled uncertainly at the deputy. "Sorry, Officer," he said. "I didn't mean to interrupt anything. I was just coming to chat with these ladies for a moment."

"That's okay," Ainsworth said. "I was actually wanting to talk to you." He stepped forward and put a hand on Crenshaw's arm. "Why don't you come on downstairs with me now?"

Crenshaw paled and swallowed hard. "Um, can't it wait?"

"No, I don't think it can," Ainsworth said. As I watched, his grasp tightened on Crenshaw's arm, and

Crenshaw winced. "Ladies, if you'll excuse us, Mr. Crenshaw and I have some business to discuss."

"Certainly," I said, and Sophie and Marylou also said something. I wasn't really listening to what they said. Instead I was focused on Haskell Crenshaw's face. He knew what was about to happen, and he was terrified.

In that moment I felt really sorry for him. He caught me looking at him, and he must have read my feelings in my expression. For a moment, he offered me a sad smile. The smile faded, and he took a deep breath.

"Okay, Deputy," Crenshaw said. "I'm ready to go."

Ainsworth nodded. He escorted Crenshaw to the door. "Ladies," he said, inclining his head before he left.

The door closed behind them. Marylou, Sophie, and I sat there in silence for a long moment.

"He really had me fooled earlier," Sophie said. "He had me convinced that Basil Dumont killed Avery."

"Me, too," Marylou said. "I still can't quite take it all in."

"He was a very good actor," Sophie said.

"About some things, maybe," I sighed.

"What do you mean?" Marylou asked.

"I think he really cared for Avery," I said. "In fact, I think he's the only one besides Will who did." I paused for a moment. "You remember the old saying about how a man kills the thing he loves most?"

"That's really sad." Sophie shook her head.

We contemplated that in silence until Marylou spoke again. "Do you think we can go home tomorrow?"

"I don't know," I said. "We probably should ask the deputy first."

"I really would like to go home right now," Sophie said.

"I would, too," I said. "I know just how you both feel. But maybe we can go home tomorrow."

"What should we do in the meantime?" Sophie asked.

Marylou had an odd expression on her face. Sophie and I laughed.

"I know, I know," I said. "Play bridge." I got up from the sofa. "You're right, Marylou—we might as well. I can't think of anything better to help pass the time."

That's just what we did. As always, bridge was the perfect distraction.

Emma Diamond's Bridge Tips

Bidding is a crucial part of the game. Partners have to communicate with each other during the bidding process, and ending up with a good contract is the outcome of successful bidding (i.e., successful communication). Sometimes the bidding process is easy and the path to the final contract smooth. Such is the nature of bridge, however, that bidding can be like tiptoeing through a minefield.

Here is an example of a relatively easy bidding process.

You have just dealt the hand, and you assemble your cards to see whether you can bid. You hold

♠ A K J 9 6
♥ K 7 4
♦ Q 10 2
♣ J 3

You have fourteen high card points, with five spades. With this hand you would open with a bid of one spade. Your left-hand opponent passes, and your partner contemplates her hand. She holds

♠ 10 8 7 2
♥ Q J 2
♦ A 9 8 5
♣ K 10

She has ten high card points and four spades to an honor. With this hand she would respond with a bid of two spades. Her left-hand opponent also passes, and now you have to reassess your hand with the information your partner has given you.

With a response of two spades, you know your partner is telling you that she has six to ten points and spade support. If she is on the low side (six points), then together you have twenty high card points. This is not enough for game. If she has ten points, you have a combined twenty-four points. Again, this isn't quite enough for game. For a game bid (in this case four spades) in a major suit you need a combined total of twenty-six points. With twenty-four points you're a bit short. You might make three spades, but more than likely you will stop the bidding at two spades.

With those two hands the bidding process is fairly clear. What do you do in a situation where the process isn't clear at all? For example, you have this hand

♠ J 7 4
♥ A K 8
♦ Q 9 6 5
♣ K 10 2

You have fourteen high card points, but your best suit is four diamonds to the queen. Opening with a four-card minor can be dodgy, and you don't have enough points to open one no-trump, even though you have a balanced hand with an honor in every suit.

In situations like this, if you are the first to bid (whether as the dealer or because those bidding before you have passed), you can open with a one club bid. This is the minimum bid you can make. It is quite common to use the one club bid as a way of telling your partner that you have opening points, but that you don't have a suit to bid. You might have a legitimate one club bid, with five or more clubs, but your partner won't know that unless you have a chance to rebid the clubs.

Your partner has heard the one club bid, there is no intervening bid, and now she must decide how to respond. If she has a particularly weak hand, with five or fewer high card points, theoretically she should pass because she doesn't really have enough points to bid. That could leave you in a bad situation if you don't have a legitimate club opener and there is no intervening bid. At this point some players make use of the "diamond bust" bid. In other words, your partner would bid one diamond to indicate that she has a very poor hand with little or no support for you. By bidding one diamond, she at least gives you the opportunity to bid again if you need to (for example, if you have a four-card major that you could bid instead or if you want to try a one no-trump bid).

If your partner has six to ten points and a good diamond suit, she would bid two diamonds to show you that she has more than a "bust" hand. If she has six to ten points and a five-card major suit, she would bid one in that suit. The one club bid is often interpreted by the partner as an invitation to name her best suit. If she is able to name a major suit, and you're able to support that bid, you can play the contract in a major suit.

The one club opener can be a very useful—and a

very frustrating—bid. If you and your fellow bridge players decide to use the one club opener and the diamond bust response, you should discuss it before beginning play to ensure that everyone understands. Otherwise you could end up with some very confused bidding if some people understand what's going on and others don't.

Another useful convention in bidding is the use of transfers in response to a one no-trump opener. In chapter 13 Bob and Bart give Emma and Sophie an explanation of this, and you might want to reread this section as a refresher on transfers.

Bidding is a tricky process, and we've just touched on some of the basics here. There is much more to learn, and for those who want to know more about the intricacies of bidding and responding, Emma (and I) recommend the following books:

- Silberstang, Edwin. *Handbook of Winning Bridge*. 2nd ed. Cooper Station, NY: Cardoza Publishing, 2003.
- Grant, Audrey. *Bidding*. ACBL Bridge Series. Memphis: American Contract Bridge League, 1990.

If you would like to know more about Emma Diamond and the Bridge Club series, please check out the Web site www.bridge-mysteries.com

About the Author

Honor Hartman is the pseudonym for a mystery author who has lived in Houston, Texas, for more than twenty-five years, has two cats and thousands of books, and plays bridge as often as possible.

A PEACH OF
A MURDER

A Fresh Baked Mystery

LIVIA J. WASHBURN

*Fresh out of the oven: the first in a new series
of baking mysteries. Includes recipes!*

All year round, retired schoolteacher Phyllis Newsom is
as sweet as peach pie—except during the Peach
Festival, whose blue ribbon has slipped through
Phyllis's fingers more than once...

Everyone's a little shook up when the corpse of a
no-good local turns up underneath a car in a local
garage. But even as Phyllis engages in some amateur
sleuthing, she won't let it distract her from out-baking
her rivals and winning the upcoming
Peach Festival contest.

With her unusual Spicy Peach Cobbler, Phyllis hopes to
knock 'em dead. But that's just an expression—never in
her wildest dreams did she think her cobbler would
actually kill a judge. Now, she's suspected of murder—
and she's got to bake this case wide open.

**Available wherever books are sold or
at penguin.com**

Penguin Group (USA) Online

What will you be reading tomorrow?

Tom Clancy, Patricia Cornwell, W.E.B. Griffin,
Nora Roberts, William Gibson, Robin Cook,
Brian Jacques, Catherine Coulter, Stephen King,
Dean Koontz, Ken Follett, Clive Cussler,
Eric Jerome Dickey, John Sandford,
Terry McMillan, Sue Monk Kidd, Amy Tan,
John Berendt…

You'll find them all at
penguin.com

*Read excerpts and newsletters,
find tour schedules and reading group guides,
and enter contests.*

Subscribe to Penguin Group (USA) newsletters
and get an exclusive inside look
at exciting new titles and the authors you love
long before everyone else does.

PENGUIN GROUP (USA)
us.penguingroup.com